LONG GONE

LONG GONE

PREDATORS AND PROTECTORS

CHRIS R. JONES

TATE PUBLISHING
AND ENTERPRISES, LLC

Published by Tate Publishing & Enterprises, LLC
127 E. Trade Center Terrace | Mustang, Oklahoma 73064 USA
1.888.361.9473 | www.tatepublishing.com

Tate Publishing is committed to excellence in the publishing industry. The company reflects the philosophy established by the founders, based on Psalm 68:11,
"The Lord gave the word and great was the company of those who published it."

Book design copyright © 2015 by Tate Publishing, LLC. All rights reserved.
Cover design by Maria Louella Mancao
Interior design by Angelo Moralde
Illustrations by: Rob Dumo | www.RobDumoArt.com

Published in the United States of America

ISBN: 978-1-68118-045-8
Fiction / Thrillers / Crime
15.03.11

Dedicated to my family.

Prologue

When I was ten years old, I had a fever. I stayed home from school and was lying on the couch in the living room as my mother cared for me. Falling in and out of sleep, feeling hot then cold, hungry and then nauseous, I dozed off in my feverish state. I had a brief dream. The dream was of hundreds of tiny circles that danced around on a snowy white surface. They were alive somehow and were pure and innocent. They seemed to be sort of playing together happily. They were also fragile, like small bubbles or tiny, hollow glass balls. Unfortunately, they were also oblivious and unaware of the fate that approached them. I, however, as a spectator, was well aware of what was coming.

Somewhere in the distance of my mind, a giant wave of much larger balls approached. They rumbled like thunder as they marched forward. Although I had not seen them yet, somehow I knew that they were unstoppable. They outnumbered the smaller orbs one hundred to one and were easily ten times their size. The large balls were gray, heavy, and rock solid. Completely different from the tiny glass-like balls they approached. They rolled over each other, making the loud thundering noise, and destroyed everything in their path. They left dust and ash in their wake. They were coming and could not—would not—be stopped. Faster and closer, they approached the small balls. Were they evil or maybe just uncaring? Perhaps it's the same thing.

The thundering sound of the gray balls approaching grew louder and louder. I knew that eventually, they would run the small balls over, crushing them all. The small balls could not hear the rumbling, even though, to me, the sound was deafening. I wished I could warn the innocent ones, but it was impossible as they were in my head but distant at the same time. They were in a world that I could not enter. I could only helplessly observe it take place. They were going to die. It was an unjust tragedy, and it seemed as if my brain was boiling.

I woke in a sudden sweat, thankful that it was over. Was it a dream and the balls never really existed at all? Was this great evil happening out there in some alternate world? Was it all just madness within my head?

I wondered which was worse.

1

The light shines in the darkness,
and the darkness has not understood it.

—John 1:5

Friday, June 5

_____

The girls were playing a game called "Table Talk," where you draw a card from the deck and read a random question from the card to be discussed among the players. It was nothing more than a way to start a conversation really and with Amy being as shy as she was, not a terrible idea.

"So who is your hero?" Jessica asked Amy.

"Um…I don't really know."

"Really?"

"Um…yeah, I don't know. I guess I really don't have a hero…I don't know."

"Well, that's weird," Jessica said.

Amy was silent.

Noticing Amy's discomfort, Dave, Jessica's dad, chimed in, "You know who my hero is?"

"No, who, Dad?" Jessica asked.

Amy just looked at him.

"You guys are my heroes."

"What?" Jessica snickered. "Oh yeah, right, Dad!"

Amy's eyes went to the floor. She sat silently.

What Dave said was directed more toward Amy than his own daughter, but he didn't want to single her out and embarrass her.

He had seen Amy from time to time around the apartments and would say hello, but she would never make eye contact with him. He couldn't blame her for that though; these days, pretty much every kid in the US was taught not to talk to strangers, especially adults.

She lived with her aunt in the apartment across from his own. When she was just three years old, she'd lost both her parents in the same car accident that had left her with a spinal injury and partial paralysis in her left leg. The injury caused her to walk sort of funny, almost sideways. It reminded Dave of the kids starring in those terrible 1970s grade school films he'd been forced to watch about scoliosis. *Get in line. Let's check your spine.* Those horror movies would make any kid sit up straight for at least a week.

Dave arrived home from work one afternoon and saw her coming up the sidewalk on her way home from school. She accidentally dropped her schoolbooks, and they scattered in all directions. He went over to help her gather her things, straightened everything up as well as he could, smiled, and handed it all back to her gently. She said a shy "Thank you" and quickly walked away.

Later that day, Amy's aunt came by to thank him. She and Amy knew Dave as their new neighbor, but no proper introductions had ever taken place. Her aunt explained that she was the older sister of Amy's mother and told him about the car accident that had injured Amy and taken her parents. She also told him what a difficult time Amy was having in school because kids would tease her about her limping.

It was heartbreaking. During the conversation, Dave had considered telling a little of his own story, but after hearing all of that, he decided against it. He felt really bad for Amy, so he thought it would be nice to order up some pizza, ask her over to watch a movie, and let her hang out with Jessica. She and Jessica seemed to get along just fine.

Now, here he was, opening his big mouth, hoping to encourage her a little.

"I'll tell you why you're my heroes," he began.

Jessica leaned forward, feigning wide-eyed interest. "Oh, do tell!" she said sarcastically.

Amy watched Jessica with a shy smile, a little amused by her antics.

"Well…you're my heroes because I remember what it was like being in ninth grade. With all the kids in school trying to be all cool and everything, I wondered if I would ever fit in at all. I didn't have many friends and wasn't much good at making them either. I guess I was pretty shy. I don't really know why. I just was."

Amy sat on the couch next to Jessica, looking at the floor.

Jessica, however, looked her dad right in the eye. He smiled at her; she seemed to understand that he was hoping to encourage Amy, even if just a little.

"So," Dave continued, "after a while, I just didn't want to even go to school. I didn't mind my teachers and stuff, but all those jerky kids there…well…I just hated it. Of course, my parents made me go, and over time, I made a few friends and things were fine, but at first, it was pretty hard just to drag my butt in there…"—he paused, realizing he was losing his train of thought—"so I have a lot of respect for you girls. Being a high school freshman is really tough, and I know there are days you don't want to go, but you *do* go, every day."

Both the girls were looking at him now; he definitely had their attention, so he went on. "It's just kind of a hard thing to do when you're not a big bad football player, or a cheerleader, or one of the popular kids, or whatever. When you are new, or a little shy like I was, it's hard. It takes a lot of guts to walk those halls."

Amy went back to looking at the floor.

He tried to finish a little more lightheartedly. "So bam! There you have it! That makes you guys my heroes!"

Jessica smiled and Dave smiled back. There was an uncomfortable pause; he didn't know what to say next.

Jessica, maybe sensing his discomfort, spoke up, "There's just one problem with all of that, Dad."

He just looked at her, waiting for her to finish her thought.

"We're girls."

He wasn't sure what she meant. "Okay. And…?"

"We can't be heroes."

"What? Well, of course you can. Anyone can be—"

"No," she said smartly, "we're *heroines*."

"Oh, good grief"—he laughed—"so sue me!"

"Just sayin'…" she teased.

"Yeah, okay, thanks, I got it."

Amy had her hands over her face, trying to control her giggling.

"Okay, heroes…oh, excuse me…*heroines*, I'm going to go on to bed and leave you two alone now to watch your movie, or whatever it is that heroines do. Amy, you can stay as long as you like." He got up from the chair and headed for the hallway, toward his bedroom.

"Dad?"

He turned. "Yes, my dear?"

"You're weird."

Amy started giggling again.

"Okay…G'nite, girls!"

Dave stopped in the little hallway bathroom to brush his teeth. He then took a quick look at his face in the mirror. His eyes looked tired, but his mind was alive. He knew he would have trouble falling asleep—again. He went to his room crawled into bed. As predicted, he stayed awake for at least two hours, tossing and turning, thinking of Kathy, then finally, falling asleep.

2

Blessed are the meek:
for they shall inherit the earth

—Matthew 5:5

June 6

"Hey, kiddo, we better get going."

"All right, Dad, I'll be out in a second."

Probably making sure her hair's perfect. Never can look good enough for a plane ride. Dave smiled at the thought, grabbed her bags, and headed out to place them in the trunk of his car. It seemed a lot of stuff for such a short visit, especially when all she wore were T-shirts, shorts, and sandals the whole time. Her mother must have helped her pack. She was the ultimate overpacker, and it used to drive him nuts.

He put her things in the trunk and went back into the apartment. *She's so grown up for a fourteen. Doing her own hair and makeup...everything. She didn't do that for herself just a little while back when we all lived together.*

Jessica exited the bathroom and smiled at him. "All right, Dad, let's hit it!"

I'm gonna miss her. I miss her already. "Okeydoke, let's go," he said as they stepped out of the apartment, and got into his car. It was a day pretty much like every other summer day in Boise, hot.

"You looking forward to getting back to Denver?" he asked

"Yeah, I guess so. It's okay there."

"Why, you got a boyfriend waiting or something?"

"Uh…yeah, sure, right, Dad," she said, rolling her eyes.

He laughed. "Well, just remember there are two kinds of—"

"I know. I know," she interrupted. "Two kinds of boys in this world, predators and protectors. I know, Dad. You've told me, like, a thousand million times."

He smiled at her. "Well, glad to see it has sunk in then."

She smiled back. "I guess this makes it a thousand million and one."

"I guess so," he said, "but then, who's counting?"

He suddenly felt a pit in his stomach. *I love her so much… and her mom.*

It was mostly a quiet drive, and a short one. He had always joked that everything in Boise was only twenty minutes away. Heck, it was true.

They turned into the airport driveway. Different signs hung over the road, telling you which lanes were for what. He got in the lane marked SHORT-TERM PARKING.

"You don't need to park, Dad. Just drop me off," she stated, knowing what the response would be.

"Um…no," he said.

Airport drop-offs were for coworkers and in-laws, not your own child.

Jessica laughed, rolling her eyes again. "Have it your way then."

"You mean like Burger King?"

"Burger King? What does that mean?"

"Never mind, it's from an old TV ad. You know, from way back in the '90s."

"Oh wow, that *was* a long time ago," she teased.

He turned into the parking garage and easily found a spot on the first level.

Slow day at BOI. He walked with her to get her ticket, then on to the security checkpoint, where all the good-bye's took place. *This is where it gets tough.* He grabbed her by the shoulders, looking into her eyes. "I love you, sweetheart. Have a safe trip." He pulled her in and hugged her as his eyes welled up.

"I love you too, Dad," she said, looking up. "I'll see you again soon, okay?"

"Okay, honey, thanks for visiting, and tell your mom I said…um…I, uh…tell her I, uh, said hello."

"I will." She looked him in the eyes. "I love you, Dad."

He smiled at her, and they hugged once more. *She feels sorry for me. I don't like my own daughter feeling sorry for me, that's for sure.* He kissed her on the top of her head and watched as she went through security.

She took her flip-flops off and placed them and her carry-on bag on the conveyor to run through the scanner. The security guy smiled at her and invited her through the detector—no beeps. She gathered her things on the other side, threw her flip-flops on the floor, stepped into them, and looking back, smiled and waved. He waved back and watched her disappear around the corner on her way back to Denver. He turned around, took a deep sighing breath, and headed right back out to his lonely life.

When he reached his car, he got in, put the key in the ignition, but didn't start it up. *Saturday. What time is it?* He looked at the car clock on the radio display. *Just after noon. Jessie will be boarding her plane pretty soon.*

Saturday. There was a time when he relished this day, relished the whole weekend; now it was mostly just long hours of being bored, with nothing to do. *I sure do miss Kathy. I miss us all being together in that house.* At least when he was alone in the old house, he could mess around in the garage, work on a car, or mow the lawn or something. Living in an apartment in downtown Boise, he found himself feeling cooped up. He didn't have to be cooped up, of course. He just didn't have the desire or energy to go do anything.

He didn't want to bother any of his friends. When you're forty years old, or close enough, hanging out with friends on the weekends is pretty much out, unless. *Hey, maybe one of them could get divorced too. Well, legally separated anyway, then we could hang out. What does that mean, legally separated? Is there illegal separation?*

He put his head down on the steering wheel as if exhausted, his mind wandering back to better times, times he'd underappreciated. Now he was alone, feeling sorry for himself; it was pitiful, really. *Snap out of it! It's summer! Go fishing. Go golfing. I suck at golf. I hate golf! Go for a drive then. Go camping. Do something! Anything!*

Suddenly there was a loud crashing noise, and the whole car shook. *Something hit the back of my car!* He snapped his head up to see what was going on, caught a red flash in his rear view and jerked around to see a pickup pulling away. He jumped out and ran back behind the car, watching the red truck drive off. *Is this guy not going to stop?* In disbelief, he spoke aloud, "That guy just hit me!"

The guy wasn't speeding away though, just driving normally through the lot and up to the ramp to the next level.

He probably didn't even realize there was someone sitting in the car. How many people just sit in their cars at the airport feeling sorry for themselves? Dave began running after the truck, then stopped and headed back to his car. *Not many, I guess. I hope.*

His trunk was slightly dented, and a taillight was shattered. He noticed a broken red-and-amber plastic on the cement parking lot floor as he ran around to the driver's side. He jumped in, started the car, and cut a sharp arc out of the parking space, and headed up to the second level. *Where did he go? There he is!* The red truck was across the lot, heading up the ramp to the third level. *Looks like it's a little Chevy.* Dave went after him.

When he got up to the third level, the lot was nearly empty, except for a few cars parked near the elevator access. The red truck was pulling into a parking space among them. He could see it good now. *Yep, it's a Chevy S-10.* He drove slowly across the lot, his eyes on the cab of the Chevy. The driver looked to be a man of about his age, maybe a little younger, thirty-five or so. There was damage to the front driver's side fender, white paint from his own car imprinted on the red truck.

Dave stopped about one hundred feet back and watched. *What is he doing in there?* The guy hadn't noticed him yet. He was looking down, fooling with something on the seat beside him. *Maybe he has a gun!* Dave waited and watched intently. *What's this guy doing?* The man lifted his hand up, and Dave could see he had a hamburger. *A hamburger!* Switching the burger into his left hand, the man lifted a large soda cup with his right and took long draw on the straw sticking up through the center of the cup.

Feeling pretty nervous, Dave got out of his car and walked toward the truck. He could see the man was probably more like in his late twenties. He had a fat face, pale skin, long wiry brown hair, and some awful-looking bushy sideburns. There was something wrong with his ears. He didn't see it at first because of the long hair, but now he could see his ear lobes were dangling. It was like loose dead skin hanging behind those sideburns. He must've had those big ridiculous hoops in his ears at one time, and now they were absent. It looked disgusting. *Why do people do that to themselves?*

He was just an all-around kind of a messy guy, *a* fat slob, for the lack of a better term. The man noticed Dave approaching and rolled down his window, ready to talk it seemed. Beside him sat a large blue-canvas duffel and a McDonald's bag. *McDonald's, of course.* Dave could smell the familiar french fry grease that couldn't be mistaken for anything else on the planet but McDonald's.

"Hey, man, what are you doing?" he asked, as the man lifted the soda straw to his lips again.

"What," the man said, not a question, but a statement.

I can see where this is going. "You hit my car down there."

"No, I didn't."

"What?" Dave tried to keep his cool. *Are you kidding me?* "Yeah! Take a look at your fender!" He motioned with his head toward his own car. "When you came around the corner down there, you clipped the back of my car!"

The guy casually looked back at Dave's car. "What's that, a Ford Focus? Who cares?"

Who cares? Okay, this is getting irritating. Dave could feel his heart pounding harder. *Yeah, it's a Focus. What's your point, dirtbag?* He took a deep breath. *Blessed are the meek.*

It was the first part of the verse of the day, from a daily Bible verse e-mail he'd read earlier that morning. *Blessed are the meek.* He took another long deep breath and was about to reply when the man spoke again.

"Look, dude, I don't have time for this right now. I got a plane to catch." The man took a bite of his burger and had mustard in his beard. *I could punch you for that alone. Wipe off your face, you slob!* Dave took another deep breath. *Blessed are the meek. Okay, I'll just get the guy's driver's license number and insurance stuff. My car's not too badly damaged.*

"Okay, c'mon, let's just, let's…Just give me your info and…and…um…we can work it out later." *After all, his truck's right here. It should be all right.*

"Yeah, whatever," the man said, looking around the cab of the pickup. "I don't have a pen, dude."

"I do. I'll grab one, just a sec," Dave turned and jogged back his car. *I better grab a piece of paper and make sure I write it all down myself too. Don't need to have all this written down on a dirty napkin, that is, if this guy would even bother using a napkin.*

He was leaning over, digging though the center console, when he heard a door shut. He sat up and looked over toward the little red pickup. The man was out and had the duffel bag over his shoulder. He was carrying the extra large soda in one hand, supersized burger and McDonald's bag in the other. *What's he doing now?* The man turned and started walking toward the elevators, his underwear showing over the top of his baggy jeans.

Dave got out of his car and with as much authority as he could muster, yelled, "Hey!" The man didn't turn but raised his soda cup in the air and waved it. That fat red straw sticking up looked a lot, to Dave, like it was giving him the finger. Head hot and heart pounding, his mind swooned and something instantly shifted in his skull. He saw injustice, he saw divorce, he saw rapists stalking the streets while cops ate doughnuts, he saw child abuse, and he saw starving children. *Children this jerk's probably stealing hamburgers from!* He saw it all, dressed in dirty baggy jeans and giving him the finger.

He saw red,—blood red. Eyes burning with hatred, he ran toward the man.

With Dave gaining speed and closing fast, the scum of the earth casually walked on toward the elevator. The slob heard him coming and was starting to turn when Dave dropped his shoulder and connected it with the lowlife's ribcage, just under his soda arm. Dave drove him hard into a rough cinder-block wall as ice and cold soda exploded into the air, riding him down to the cement floor where they landed nearly face-to-face. The dirtbag lay still; Dave could feel the scum's chin on the top of his own head.

That nasty mustard beard…those dangling ear lobes!

Dave jumped to his feet to stand over him.

The man groaned and looked up dizzily until their eyes finally met. Dave could see, even feel, the fear enter the man's eyes. *He's paralyzed with fear!* This sent a surge of adrenaline through his body like he had never felt before. His anger was uncontrollable; there would be no ignoring him this time.

He glared down and yelled, "You like that? Huh? You like that? I oughta beat the crap out of you! You crash into my car and then do this?"

Frightened, mouth open, and breathing heavy, the man lay still, just staring. His gaze was as if he were about to utter his last words, mustard and ketchup smeared on his face and down his dirty shirt.

Dave stood panting. *Man, are you ugly!* His anger not subsiding in the least, he felt that he had to do more. He had to release this anger. He looked around—the floor was wet with soda and quickly melting ice, the McDonald's bag lay open with french fries spilling out, and what was left of the hamburger was lying next to the man's open hand. Adrenaline pumping, Dave grabbed the burger off the concrete floor and leaned over the man's head, staring into his eyes intently. The man recoiled, as much as he could anyway. *Frozen with fear. Good!*

Shoving the rest of the hamburger into the slobs gaping mouth, Dave lowered his voice. "Yeah, you like that, don't you?" The man coughed, gagged, and tried to turn his face away as Dave shoved it in harder. "Yeah, you *do* like that, don't you? Eat up now, bud. C'mon now, eat it all up." The man's head rested in complete submission on the concrete floor, hamburger parts protruding from his piehole.

Breathing heavy, heart still pounding hard, Dave stood up, looked around, and somewhat came to his senses. "Don't miss your flight now, buddy."

He jogged back to his car and jumped in. He began fumbling with the keys because his hands were shaking uncontrollably. He managed to settle himself down enough to get the key in the ignition and fire up the car, and off he went.

3

Detective Matthew Carr stood outside behind the Boise police station, rocking a foil wrapped piece of gum between his fingers, looking out toward the Rockies. His mind was fixed on two local kids who were missing from a campground out by Hells Canyon. The two girls, high school juniors, had been rafting on the Snake River with a senior named Aaron Reed. The story was that they were all rafting together when Aaron jumped out and swam to shore. He then walked back to the campground, leaving the girls alone in the raft. Apparently, this was all because he didn't feel like walking all the way back to the pullout spot farther down the river. *Would have been nice of you to stay with the girls, idiot.* That was two days earlier. Emma Mitchell and Caitlyn Peterson hadn't been seen since. He unwrapped the gum, put it in his mouth, and chewed on it aggressively.

Those girls likely drowned. Still early summer. Water's high and fast. Be a small miracle to locate them in the Snake right now. It was a big story in the news, with all the reporters dragging their camera crews out to the river and talking about summer safety and whatnot. They were trying anything to get interviews with those poor kids' parents, their friends, and whoever would talk. It was a circus. *What would the press do without tragedy?*

The search party would soon lose hope and give up. Their bodies would probably turn up down river in a couple months. Unfortunately, that was the reality of the situation; every summer, kids were drowning in the rivers and in irrigation canals in the valley. He'd seen so much of it through the years that it seemed like just a part of life here.

Anyway, he was in homicide and had been sent to interview the Aaron kid; he'd done his part and saw no foul play. *Not really my problem now.*

A fellow officer poked his head out the back door. "Hey, Matt, we got a call for you in here."

Matt dropped the silver wrapper into a big stone ashtray that was by the back door of the police station. The wrapper and many others just like it were slowly covering up his old cigarette butts in there. He had quit smoking, again, about a month ago. He didn't necessarily like the reminder of the butts in the ashtray. It was the smell that got to him and tempted him. *Maybe the janitor will clean them up one day. Maybe I'll find a new hangout.*

"What is it?" Matt asked, turning toward the door

"They need you out at the airport, pronto."

4

"Get in!" he said. "Get in the car!" He pushed the kid head first into the cab of the old pickup and slammed the door. He really didn't need to say a word. The kid was out cold and couldn't hear him anyway.

He went around the other side, opened the driver's door, and got in. He then turned toward his new passenger. "Maybe I should kill you, and maybe I will."

Then he started the truck and drove off. It was a good plan he had come up with. Not just good, it was a great plan. Stick to the plan. Soon they would find the kid's car, and things would start to turn his way. The plan is good. *I'm a genius, Gary the genius*, he told himself. *Gary the genius.* He liked the way that sounded because it rhymed.

5

Dave stood outside his apartment building assessing the damage to his car. *A Ford Focus. Who cares?* The trunk was dented pretty good, actually. It was worse than he first thought. Red paint was smeared across it. It would be easiest to just replace the whole trunk lid. The bumper also had red paint on it and cracks in the white paint where the bumper had flexed, but it wasn't a big deal. *Not bad, really. Car's not in that great of shape anyway. New trunk lid and a taillight and it'll be fine.*

He was still shaking from what happened at the airport and couldn't believe that he had lost his mind like that. *If anyone had it coming, it was that guy. I wonder if he'll call the cops.* He couldn't get the image of the guy's face out of his head. *And to jam a hamburger in his mouth, what was that all about?* He shook his head in disbelief at himself and walked the short walk to his apartment door.

When he got inside, he headed directly to the fridge, grabbed a bottled water, and sat down at the little bar thing between the kitchen and dining room, or what's considered a dining room anyway. He had no kitchen table, as he saw no reason to get one.

It's quiet without Jessica here. Though her visit was short, it was nice having the company. She never asked about the separation between him and her mother; he figured that maybe she got the story from her mom. *I hope not.* He'd wanted to bring it up while she was here to set the story straight, but he just couldn't; it was too embarrassing and awkward, and he'd just wanted to enjoy her visit.

He thought about the slob at the airport. *I wonder if he made his flight.* The thought seemed absurd. *Why the hell do I care?*

He wondered how long the incident would be on his mind like this. It had been so long since he experienced anything so intense that it seemed foreign to him. He felt a little more alive from it all. *That guy's face. Man, that was really something!* However, beating people up and jamming burgers in their mouths was not about to become his new hobby.

He figured he better take a shower and get some different clothes on. His shirt was stained with cola. He got up. *I'll go take that shower now. It might help me relax. Besides, there's nothing else to do on a Saturday.*

6

When Detective Carr arrived at the airport parking garage, traffic cops had the third level closed off but waved him on through. There were four other squad cars at the scene and another unmarked Crown Vicky like his. That would be Detective John Weatherford's car. Matt liked him; he was a good cop, new to homicide just a couple years before.

Matt got out of his car. Detective Weatherford was looking at a man lying on the ground and at the area surrounding him. The other officers stayed back and looked on. Two of them were interviewing a woman. He walked over to them first. "What's happening guys? Got a witness?"

"No, sir, she just found him here, just like that," one of the officers replied.

The woman spoke up excitedly, "I just came out of the elevator, turned the corner, and there he was lying there! I about died when I saw him, you know? I almost stepped on him! So I called 911 and waited here until these guys—"

Matt interrupted her, "Thank you, ma'am, you've been very helpful. Guys, get her on her way as soon as you can, okay?"

"Yes, sir," the two cops replied in almost perfect unison and continued taking her statement.

Matt shifted his attention to John and to the man lying on the floor next to a large duffel bag. John looked up as he approached.

"Whatchya got, John?"

"Dead man, that's for sure. No blood though, no wound that I can see. Haven't looked too much…waiting on you."

No blood, huh. "How long?"

"My guess is an hour or so. Cement's still wet from that spilled soda. Hot day too. I got here ten minutes ago. These guys already were up here"—referring to the uniformed officers—"but didn't touch anything."

Matt stepped in to take a closer look. "He's got a cheeseburger shoved in his mouth."

"Yeah, weird, huh. What do you think of that?" John asked, as he himself really had no idea what to make of it.

"I don't know. Let's look." Matt pulled a pair of rubber gloves from his waist pack and put them on. He crouched down over the man, then paused and looked up at John. "How did he get here?"

"I'm pretty sure he came in that little red pickup over there. It's unlocked, the window's down, and it's got a pile of McDonald's condiment packs on the seat. Damage on the front driver's side looks like it was recently in a fender bender. I've got one of the guys running the plates on it now."

"Good, good. We'll have a look at that, but for now, let's…" Matt's voice faded as he lifted the man's head slightly with his rubber-gloved hand and turned it so he could look at the face directly. The man's eyes were still open, and his skin still felt slightly warm. *John's right…about an hour… maybe two.* He studied the face, and the mouth essentially pried open with a cheeseburger. "See that?" He turned the face toward John.

"You mean the bun there?" Weatherford asked.

"Yeah, it's got a big dent in it. Looks like it was pushed in with someone's finger or thumb."

"Yeah, sure does. What do you think, Matt? Someone killed him and then jammed that in his mouth?" He paused. "Maybe he choked on it. No, you think?"

Killed him? Matt didn't think the burger was blocking the airway enough to suffocate him; he could always breathe through his nose. There's no mistaking that when someone is shot or stabbed, there will be blood, usually lots of it. *No blood here…none.* "I don't know." *Autopsy*, he thought.

He lifted the man's head and examined the throat; no damage there that he could see.

He felt the top of the dead man's head with his other hand. *What's this?* He pulled the hair back. The skin was red and scraped, but not bleeding. *Maybe someone cracked him over the head with a baseball bat, but the bump's not that distinct.* "Good-sized lump on his head. Check it out."

John slipped on his own gloves and felt the man's head. "Yeah, a good lump, but more like one from a fall, not from being struck with something, huh?"

Matt was impressed. *Exactly right.* "Definitely, John, you got it. It's scraped up a bit too."

John felt a bit proud of himself. It was good to impress a vet like Matt, even if just a little.

The two men looked at each other, trying to solve the riddle. They knew a small trip and fall wouldn't cause a bump like that. They both looked up, but there was really no place to fall from, and why would he park here, if he came in that truck, then go up a level to fall back down? It really didn't make much sense.

Then Matt saw it on the wall. *Mustard.* He let the man's head down gently and stood up, John's eyes following his. "Here…mustard on the wall…and some ketchup too. See?"

They examined the wall closely, trying to determine where the man's head would have hit. The wall was rough cinder block, just the sort that would scrape your head if you ran into it.

"Here it is, right here." Matt pointed to two hairs stuck in the grit of the wall.

"Yeah, looks like he slammed into the wall pretty good," John agreed. "He must have fell into it as this is only what, four feet off the ground or so? Enough force to kill him?"

"I dunno, hard to say." *Autopsy*, Matt thought again.

As they stood silently studying the wall, one of the uniformed officers approached. "Sir, we have info on the Chevy S-10. Sir?"

"What is it?" John asked

"It's registered to one Sarah DeSantis of Boise."

The detective thought for a moment and then looked at John. "I'm pretty sure this guy's not Sarah."

John knew what was coming and pulled a notepad and pen from his pack, ready to write.

"Okay," Matt said, "let's get this area taped off ASAP. We need to find the owner of that truck. I'll find out who our body is. If he was getting on a plane, he'll have an ID. I'm going to need a passenger list of all flights in and out of this place from this morning up till now."

He realized that whoever did this could still be in the airport. *How much of a stink should I make? Not likely the perp would just be hanging around here. He either got on a flight or left some other way.*

"Let's find out if anyone did short-notice flight cancellations as well."

John jotted it down.

"Also, let's check on any hit-and-run reports, white car, of course."

"Yep," John agreed.

"See if any of the cameras around this place caught anything, maybe the S-10 coming in, you know, anything," *Doubt it. The outside security system is a mess with all the construction going on.* "Oh, and check the McDonald's across the road. They probably sold him the burger. See if their cameras got something."

Not much to go on. Don't really know anything yet.

"You"—he motioned for the uniformed cop to step closer—"I need you to get a hold of the captain and get some men in the terminal. I want them on the lookout for anyone who looks like they've been in a fight. Probably has soda stains and hamburger crap all over them. Get the TSA clowns to help you if you can."

"Yes, sir. You got it…understood," the officer replied and headed for his squad car.

"And hey, keep it low-key, all right? And make sure the guys down below keep the press out of here."

"Yes, sir."

Have to deal with them soon enough. Wish I had a smoke. I mean, no I don't. He looked at John. "Let's find out who this guy is and what's in his bag."

7

Gary the genius pulled up to the main barn out behind the house. The kid still was lying silent in the passenger side of the big bench seat, his hands bound behind his back, a canvas feed bag over his head. He left the kid in the truck for now. He wasn't going anywhere. Still, he kept an eye on him as he opened the barn door. It was a large barn and at one time was full of feed for the animals. There was a loft above where he used to stack hay at the end of each harvest. The animals were all gone now, as well as the hay bales.

He turned and walked over to an old refrigerator in the corner of the barn and pulled out a beer, popped the top, and started drinking it as he marveled at his latest handiwork. *Genius.*

Inside the barn lay a large metal shipping container. It was a common thing for farmers to have them as they were excellent for storing stuff. You could even fit a small tractor in one, or a bunch of smaller pieces of equipment, parts, or even, people.

It was green, where it wasn't rusted away, and read HYUNDAI on the side of it in large white letters. He sometimes wondered what kind of stuff was originally shipped in the containers when he worked the farm.

It used to be on the outside of the barn, but he moved it into barn, by pushing it in with the only tractor he had left. He also cut some slats in the top and the sides with an oxyacetylene torch to allow some light in. The slats were long and narrow, too small for a person to get through. Inside of the container he threw in an old mattress and some blankets and pillows from the farmhouse.

He also cut a hole in the floor about a foot in diameter and dug a hole into the dirt floor of the barn with a post hole digger, a toilet, it would do. The hole even had a bucket of lime powder next to it. Finally, he ran a water hose on the barn floor with a valve on the end of it. He shoved the valve end into a slat on the metal box and then turned on the main valve at the spigot at the rear wall of the barn. Running water, what more could a person want?

It was all stuff from around the farm, a perfect apartment, and it didn't cost him a dime. In the other barn, where most of the farm equipment, now sold, used to be, another apartment very similar to this one sat. Gary the genius. Wow, it was impressive.

Of course, if that old farmer would have given the farm to Gary like he should have when he died, none of this would be necessary. After all those years of working for that old man, he gives the farm to his son. That infuriated Gary. The farmer's son never worked on the farm. He barley even visited in the twenty-five years Gary had worked there. Hardly ever once in twenty-five years! The only time he did come out was for Christmas and Thanksgiving. He also came out for the old man's funeral, but that was about it.

That guy didn't care about the farm. He was only interested in selling it. He was big city slicker out in Chicago, working for some big fancy bank. He was a jerk and Gary hated him. Hated him for being the new owner of the ten thousand acres that should be his. That jackass just wanted what Gary felt was his, *knew* was his. Gary worked had worked there forever. The farmer's son was going to sell the farm and then what? I'll tell you what. Good ol' Gary would have to go, that's what.

Until then, the farmer's son told him in a letter that he could live there for free tending to the place. He sent Gary a check once a month for food and, more importantly, beer and whiskey. It was only a matter of time before Gary would be homeless, but he had his plan, and it was all coming together. The thought of pulling it off put his mind at ease a bit. He didn't need this farm. It wouldn't be long now that he would leave this place forever.

Gary went back to collect his new tenant from the car.

8

Detective Carr was ready to face the press, as ready as he could be anyway.

The search through the airport terminal came up empty. TSA agents saw nothing to cause any suspicion. No man soaked in soda was seen in the area.

The cameras at McDonald's had good shots of the truck passing through, but only the inside camera covering the drive-through showed anything important. There was a clear and distinct shot of the dead man behind the wheel, his big blue duffel bag beside him, being led into view by an unmistakably undamaged left front fender.

They still were working on looking through some recorded videotape from airport security, maybe that would turn up something more.

He had identified the dead man as Ron Wells of Sacramento, California. Wells had come into Boise just two days earlier and clearly not with the best intentions in mind.

The truck belonged to Sarah DeSantis, an elderly widow living in north Boise. Wells had approached Mrs. DeSantis in the parking lot of a grocery store the night before. At knifepoint, he threatened her and forced her to drive them both to her house. Once there, he taped her up and packed his duffel bag with her jewelry, money, and her one credit card. Then, according to Mrs. DeSantis, he spent the night in her home watching TV and eating her food while she lay on the floor. In the morning, he casually left, leaving her there taped up. *What a freaking psycho.*

A patrol officer attempting to contact Mrs. DeSantis at home got no response but was hailed by a neighbor who'd become concerned when he saw police at her door. The neighbor had earlier noticed her garage door standing open and had closed it for her, thinking she had driven off and forgotten it again. The officer called his supervisor, who came with a battering ram and plenty of backup. They found the elderly and frail Sarah DeSantis on the floor of her living room with her hands duct-taped behind her back. More duct tape was wrapped around her head and into her mouth as a gag.

Wells was a dirtbag, that much was obvious; seems someone else knew it too and took care of business. The dead man turning out to be such a slime ball made things a bit easier for Carr to swallow. Flying into Idaho from California to rob people was nothing new. These guys could get round trip tickets on the cheap, fly in, commit their crime, and fly out. Rarely could the cops track them down. Somebody tracked down Wells though and tracked him down good, but who? Whoever it was didn't rob him; he still had with him over twelve hundred dollars of presumably DeSantis's money, not to mention more than a little bit of jewelry, including gold.

Regardless of his distaste for Wells and those like him, Carr still had a death on his hands, a possible homicide. He had some problems here he needed to sort out. He wanted to keep Sarah, the elderly victim, isolated from the press, but at the same time, her stolen truck had been found with the dead man. The media would jump to conclusions, usually the wrong ones. Were the incidents related? Is Wells part of both of them? He couldn't be sure.

He walked down the ramp from the third level of the airport garage, past a patrol car, and into a barrage of cameras and microphones to make his statement. It would be extremely vague.

9

"Hey, man, wake up. Hey, wake up," the voice whispered.

Kyle was groggy. *It's so dark in here.*

"Wake up. Who are you? Hey, man, wake up."

Kyle slowly was waking up. *Where am I?*

The voice continued, "Hey, hey, hey, wake up man."

Who's this person in my face? Kyle finally spoke, "What? Huh? Where am I?"

"Who are you?" the voice asked

"I'm…what? I'm Kyle. Where am I? Who are you!"

"Shhh…hey, be quiet, shhh…You're kidnapped. Kidnapped!"

"What?" Kyle said, trying to concentrate as best he could. "What are you talking about? Who are you?"

He still couldn't see well. It was too dark, but he could make out the form of a person sitting by him where the voice was coming from. He had a terrible headache. *What is that smell?* It smelled like one of those Port-O-Potty things at a construction site or a sports complex.

Who is this person sitting next to me? Is it the man from the road? What happened to the man on the road? Where is my car? Where am I?"

"Look, I'm telling you," the voice said seriously, "you've been kidnapped, like me, and we're…we're locked in this box."

Box? Locked in a box? Kyle looked around as best he could, his eyes now adjusting to the dark. *In a box?* "No! No! No!" He immediately stood up and shouted toward the top of the box, "Hey! Let me out of here! Get me out of here! Hey!"

"No, be quiet. He'll kill us!" the voice said in a forceful whisper. "Be quiet or he'll kill us both! He *will* kill us!"

Kyle turned toward the voice. "Who will kill us?"

"The kidnapper, he'll kill us if we yell. Oh man, I hope he didn't hear you." The voice sounded frightened, very frightened.

"What did we do? Why are?…What are?…"

"Hey, hey, I…I don't know…I've been here for about a week now, I think. I don't know what's going on. He took me off the street. I was hitchhiking."

"Hitchhiking? Who are you?"

"I'm Trip, man. I was hitching, trying to get to Nevada, and he pulled over and knocked me out with something. I don't know how…and put me in here."

"Knocked you out with something?" Kyle said. "That's what happened to me!"

He'd gotten a flat tire and was on the side of the road when a car pulled up. A man got out and asked if he needed help. A big man, a farmer-looking guy wearing overalls over a dirty white T-shirt and a greasy blue ball cap on his head.

Kyle didn't need help with the tire but the man helped anyway. He seemed happy to help, as if it was his duty as an American. He reeked of beer, but he seemed friendly enough—acted friendly, anyway. The last thing he could remember was the man holding a rag over his face—ether. The man was so strong that struggling proved useless, and then he woke up here, a prisoner.

Kyle continued, "He knocked you out with ether, I bet. He knocked me out with it too. He was helping me change a tire, and he knocked me out with ether, like starting fluid."

"Starting fluid?" Trip asked. "You mean like to start a car?"

"Yeah," Kyle said, "or a lawnmower, or whatever. It could have been something else, I guess…but you breathe enough of it, and it will make you pass out." It explained his miserable headache as well.

"Well," Trip said, "you're a white dude…"

"Huh?" Kyle paused for a moment. He could see better now that his eyes had adjusted. He could see Trip was a black kid, maybe about twenty years old. "What are you talking about?"

"I don't know, man. I thought maybe the dude grabbed me because I was black or something, but I guess not." Trip sat looking at him, sharing the silence in thought; neither had a clue what was happening.

"Who is he? What does he want?" Kyle asked

"I don't know, man, I don't know."

"Does anyone know you're here?"

"I don't know…I mean, I have no idea. I don't think so"

"Someone must know you're missing…and my car, my car, it's out there. It's on the side of the freeway." Kyle tried to make sense of it all, but couldn't. It didn't make any sense at all. He knew one thing though. He didn't like it. He thought about his mom, but mostly his little brother.

"We have got to get out of here."

He looked around at the metal box and thought, *But how?*

10

That Night

Dave had a dream. He felt as if he was half asleep, but his mind was racing. It's in some strange arena where he couldn't quite wake up fully and couldn't sleep, at least not in peace.

It's not a dream so much as a seemingly random display of images and thoughts running through his mind. The images were coming in from different directions. It was as if he had three hoops around his brain that were carrying the data and putting pictures in front of his mind's eye.

A vertical hoop brought a memory of him and his older brother as kids, walking home from Kmart with a newly purchased Kiss Alive album and road flares they had stolen during the same visit. He saw his brother pull a stolen road flare out from his tube sock.

Another memory came flying in from the right side of his mind, this one an image of Kathy. She was young, beautiful, happy, and completely in love with him. This made his heart race. *Is this my life flashing before my eyes?*

From the left, the third hoop brought an image of the man with the cheeseburger at the airport, laughing at him. *This is irritating. My beautiful wife replaced by a fat jerkwad!*

Now the hoop from the top rolled in another memory and now the right and now the left, faster and faster they came and went. *Faster and faster.* Some with no meaning at all it seemed. Some good images, some disturbing. He struggled to wake, but couldn't. The memories wouldn't let him. They wouldn't stop, unless…

In the background of this chaos was some sort of riddle. It was a riddle that promised to stop his racing mind if he could just figure it out. *I can rest if I solve the riddle. The racing of my mind will stop.* Another image flashed through his mind, this one of a Yamaha motorcycle he had as a teen. *Why? What can that mean?* He tried to concentrate on the riddle and found out it consisted of three questions.

The first question: How to turn a paper circle into a square?
Easy…Fold down four flaps creating corners.
Yes, good…correct!
This is easy.

Still his mind raced and he tried to concentrate on the next part of the riddle, the second question.

Mango is to branch, as branch is to what?
Mango…Do they grow on trees? They must be somewhere in a rain forest or something. Fruit grows on a tree…

He felt like a first grader answering the second riddle. *Mango is to branch as branch is to tree.*
Wrong.
I'm wrong? Why?
Well, because branch is to trunk, not to tree, but we'll give it to you.
Thanks. Who am I thanking. Myself? This is crazy, but if it'll stop my mind racing, I'll keep playing.

A quick dream came to his mind of riding in the back-seat of an old Chrysler car with his mom. This was an actual dream, not just a quick snapshot stuck in his memory.

The dream was quickly replaced by a memory of Jessica as a kid, playing around on the beach when he and Kathy took a trip to the Oregon coast. *This is a good memory. I wish I could hold it in place and sleep peacefully.* It's gone as quickly as it came, as his mind raced through more images and memories of seemingly random thoughts. *Will it never end? Oh yes, the riddle. That will make it stop.*

In the background of his dream, he concentrated on the riddle. It's as if he has two brains, one cycling images and dreams, and one focused on the riddle. *I need to use the one that's meant for solving the riddle and try and block out the other. Put the dream to the back.*

The third and final question: Two men, one short and one tall, are trying to reach a basketball hoop, neither man is tall enough on his own. Which is taller, the tall man with the short man on his shoulders, or the short man with the tall man on his shoulders? Which one is taller?

Huh? Won't they be the same? If one stands on the other ones head, it will be the same either way, but one sitting on the other one's shoulders is actually more difficult to figure out.

This is my dream! Shouldn't I know the answer? He could feel his heart pounding in his chest. *My God, I'm having a heart attack!*

What is taller? He assumed it must be the short man on the shoulders of the tall man, but what if the tall man couldn't support the weight of the short man. *Is the short man fat and heavy? Will he topple the tall man? Can they reach the rim? Is the object to reach the rim? No, it's about height. The reaching rim thing is just a trick. Okay, so I know that it's a trick, but I'm still not sure of the answer. I'm losing my mind.*

Again, the image of Jessica on the beach came around. He's watching her play in the sand with Kathy, they were happy, holding hands. The dream seemed to stick this time. *I can't believe it.* Finally, he began to relax. The beach was beautiful. Kathy was beautiful. He tried to look at her face again. *She's gone!* He looked for Jessica. *She's gone too. They were just here! Where are they?*

He saw them farther down the beach, walking away. They were a long way off for only being gone a short time. He called out to them and began to run toward them. They didn't hear him call out.

He tried to run faster, but his legs suddenly became heavy and he could barely move them. *What's going on!* He looked at his legs, and they were coated with sand. With each step, more sand clung to him and weighed him down. The weight became too much for him to continue walking, and he fell hopelessly to the ground. He tried screaming for Jessica and Kathy, but still they couldn't hear him. The sand was so heavy he couldn't even crawl now. It's as if he's trying to swim in wet cement. The impossibly heavy sand was working its way up his torso. He continued to scream out to Kathy and Jessica, but to no avail.

Lying on his stomach, his whole body pinned to the ground, it took all his strength to keep his head up and his eyes on the girls. The sand was on his neck and getting into his mouth and nose. He tried to spit it and blow it out, but it just kept coming. *Am I going to die here? I hate this dream!*

He fought hard to wake himself up. He grabbed at his pillows and tried to jerk himself awake. He threw the pillows around, hoping to make some noise that will wake him. He tore at the sheets. He tried to knock the alarm clock off the end table next to the bed, anything to wake himself up.

Can't Kathy tell I'm struggling and just reach over and wake me up? How can she possibly be sleeping through this?

He tried everything to wake from this nightmare before he died in it. The hoops around his mind started spinning again. It seemed some sort of torture. *What is taller? Figure it out!* He struggled and thrashed in the bed, but couldn't wake up. His body weighed a ton, and he could barely move. He struggled with all his might, finally he's able to roll himself off the bed and hit the floor hard.

He was jerked wide awake with a gasp of breath and eyes opened wide. He wasn't on the floor at all. In fact, he was right in bed with everything in order, pillows, sheets, everything. He hadn't thrashed at all, much less thrown himself off the bed. There was no end table with an alarm clock, just his cell phone on the floor. There was also no Kathy lying next to him. *Reality.* As bad as the dream was, at least it wasn't real. Real or not, it left him with his heart pounding in his chest, feeling terrible and nearly paralyzed.

Relieved it was over and he was awake, he took deep breath and lay staring at the bedroom ceiling, still thinking about the riddle and of Kathy. *I don't have to figure the riddle out, do I? No, of course not. It's stupid…ridiculous…dumb. How can my own mind do this to me? Have I no control over it at all?* He lay there thinking of the past and of all the memories that ran through his mind. *A tall man and a short man…the beach…Kathy…which is taller?* He thought about that some more. It was actually a difficult riddle to solve, as stupid as it seemed. Why would his own mind confuse and torture itself like this?

Maybe I'm going insane…maybe this is how it starts. His mind wandered in a haze until eventually and, almost reluctantly, fell back asleep.

11

For there is nothing hidden that will not be
disclosed, and nothing concealed that will not be
known or brought out into the open.

—Luke 8:17

Sunday, June 7

Kyle looked out of one of the holes in the metal box. The
sun was rising, and some light was coming into the barn
where the box was located. The barn was pretty large from
what he could make out.

There was also some sunlight coming in from above. He
looked up as high as he could from his vantage point, following the wall toward the roof. There was an opening to
the outside, and what looked like a platform. A hayloft is
what he guessed the platform was for. There really wasn't
much else to see. It was just a normal wooden barn with
a dirt floor. He could see some empty beer cans on the
floor…and what looked to be a dead mouse.

He went to the other side of the box and looked out.
That side of the box was closer to the wall of the barn. All
he could see were the vertical wooden boards that made
up the barn wall. There were some sort of rusty metal farm

tools hanging from the wall. He had no idea what any of them were for.

"Where do you think we are?" he asked Trip.

"I'm not really sure, but I've thought about it myself. I think maybe close to Idaho, but I don't know, man."

Kyle thought about that and asked, "Where were you when you were picked up?"

"I was in Oregon, in a place called Pendleton. It's pretty much in the middle of nowhere, but there's a truck stop place there. There's a casino there. I was there trying to find a ride. When I got in the truck with this guy, we were heading east on highway 84. I know it was 84."

"What happened? How did he get you?"

"He didn't get me. I got in his stupid truck because he said he was headed east. Then he pulled over, said he had to check his tire, and next thing I know, I am waking up in this place."

"He could have turned around."

"Yeah, he could have," Trip agreed, "but wherever he went, he only drove for about an hour, maybe an hour and a half."

"How do you know that?"

"My phone, I didn't know exactly what time—"

Kyle interrupted, "Your phone! You have a phone?"

"Yeah, but it's dead, man. Believe me, it's dead."

"What? Can I see it? You still have it?"

"Yeah, but it's dead, dude. No reception anyway, I tried, but anyway—"

Kyle interrupted again, "Can I see it?" He just had to see for himself.

"Sure, man, but"—Trip pulled the phone out of his back pocket and handed it to him—"it's dead."

Kyle grabbed it and tried to turn it on. He tried the power button, held down both buttons, even shook it for some reason. It was dead, that was for sure. It wasn't that he didn't believe Trip that the phone was dead. He apparently just had to experience the disappointment for himself. Of course, had it powered up and was useless anyway, that would have been a real heartbreaker. He handed it back to Trip and said, "Mine is in my car out there somewhere."

"No reception here anyway, man. I tried and tried until the battery died. Believe me, man, it sucks."

"But you saw the time on it before?" Kyle asked

"Yeah, man, I figured I got in that truck about three or so, and when I looked at my phone after waking up in here, it was just after four thirty. I sort of remember being dragged in here, so I don't think I was out much longer than the drive, ya know."

Kyle thought about where he was when his car broke down. He had just crossed the Idaho border heading toward Portland. He had done this drive before, and he knew exactly where Pendleton, Oregon was. There was a casino there. It was called Wild Horse or something like that. Between Pendleton and the Oregon-Idaho border were only a few small towns, Ontario, Baker City, and La Grande. That was pretty much it. If Trip was right, he figured they were probably around Baker City or La Grande. He wasn't sure if it mattered much where they were, but it seemed like an important thing to know.

12

Dave woke up, rubbed his eyes, looked at his phone, and put his head back down, wishing he could sleep half the day away. He knew he didn't sleep well with all that went on the day before. *That guy's face…with the hamburger jammed in his mouth. That was just unbelievable.* He actually found himself feeling sorry for the guy. He couldn't get the airport incident out of his mind, or that crazy dream. *What is taller?* He tried to clear his head of the stupid question in the dream.

What am I going to do today? He had all day to himself, and it was going to be a long one. *Maybe I'll go by the hotel for a while and just see how things are going.* He was the manager of the downtown Marriott Hotel. The assistant manager worked weekends and would have things well under control as always, but at least it would give him somewhere to go and someone to talk to. *What a sorry sap I am, thinking of going to work on my day off…pitiful.*

Sunday. I suppose I could go to church. He thought about doing that every Sunday morning, but never went. They used to go to the local community church as a family, pretty regularly, or religiously as Kathy would joke. Going alone though, with rumors going around about his separation, just didn't appeal to him all that much. It was actually one of Kathy's church friends that helped get the whole ball rolling toward their separation. *Beth…She is the last person I want to see.*

He thought of Jessica and how he needed to talk to her about what had happened between him and her mom. *Maybe I'll call her today. Maybe…* He lay there feeling sorry for himself. *This is going to be a long day.* He tried to fall back asleep, just to pass the time.

13

Gary the genius was up early. He had a lot of stuff to do. The plan was coming together very well. The news last night showed one Kyle Fulton missing. His car found on the side of the road with an apparent flat tire change in progress. Kyle Fulton, a student at Portland State University from Ogden, Utah, on his way back home to visit family. *Sorry you didn't quite make it, Kyle*, Gary thought happily. The cops had no idea where Kyle had disappeared to. Gary smiled to himself. If only there was a reward offered, but there wasn't. *Too bad, Kyle, hope you like your new home!* Gary looked out the window of the old farmhouse and at the barn. All is quiet out there. He went into the kitchen and grabbed a loaf of bread off the counter and a beer from the fridge. His trusty Mossberg shotgun was on the kitchen table, and he grabbed that too. He headed outside to the barn. He was practically strutting.

He swung open the barn doors and the barn lit up. He walked in and leaned his shotgun against the edge of the barn door, in the crease by the hinge, where it wouldn't fall over.

"Wake up, sleepyheads," he said. "Are you in there, Kyle Fulton? It's breakfast time." He smiled to himself as he strolled confidently toward the iron box where he had his "boys."

Kyle listened intently to what was going on outside there in the barn. He tried to quiet his breathing to listen closely.

Gary took the loaf of bread and tore it in half, bag and all. He took one half and reached up to one of the upper slats cut in the metal wall and dropped it in.

Kyle watched the whole thing happen. It was hard to wrap his mind around what was going on. The bread hit the floor with a light thud and two pieces fell from the bag. Kyle just stared at it. *Food? Bread?* Trip went over to pick it up

This was more than Kyle could take.

"What do you want from us?" Kyle yelled out toward his captor.

"No, shhh, don't!" Trip said quickly

"Shut up in there," Gary yelled back, "or else!"

"Or else what? You freak! Let us out of here!"

This time, Trip went over and grabbed Kyle by the shoulders. "Shut up, man! Would you please shut up?"

There was silence. Something lightly dropped to the barn floor. They could hear the man on the outside walking quickly away, then he was walking back toward their cage.

"Or else this!" Gary said, and he stuck the barrel of his shotgun through one of the slats in the box. He pointed it toward the top, making sure he wouldn't shoot the occupants inside. It wasn't time for killing, yet. He squeezed the trigger.

BOOM!

The sound was deafening inside the metal can. Twelve gauge shot ricocheted around the inside of the big shipping container. Kyle and Trip hit the floor like soldiers under attack, hands over their heads. Some of the pellets hit them, but not with enough force to penetrate their skin.

"Next one is in your head, if you don't get to shutting up. When I tell you to get shut up, you get shut up!" Gary yelled. Then he racked the slide of his shotgun, expelling the spent plastic red casing to the barn floor. He reached down to the floor not to pick up the casing, but his beer and the other half of the bread loaf. Maybe he would give it to them tomorrow if he felt like it.

Stupid kids, he thought, as he walked out of the barn and swung the large double doors closed. It wouldn't be long now. He returned into the house and sat down at the kitchen table, setting the bread and his shotgun down on top of it as he sat. He leaned his head back as he guzzled the rest of the beer. He ran the plan through his mind. He had stumbled on the plan purely by accident, really. *It was meant to be*, he figured.

When he snatched the girl from California coming through at the gas station that night, he knew she was someone famous. He had spotted her getting gas at a station that was closed, but you could still buy gas with a credit card. He pulled up to a different pump, pretending he also needed gas, even though he didn't have a credit card. She looked over at him, and he tried not to stare. He suddenly wished he was that Bon Jovi guy or someone like that. Maybe then, she would like him. Girls like her always liked that that Bon Jovi guy. Although, he did see a show on TV once, where really pretty girls like her were in love with big fat guys. He wasn't even that fat, but he did realize that he wasn't the type these kind of girls fell in love with. *But maybe…*

She turned back to watch the numbers scroll on the gas pump. She had long blonde hair with some sort of green headband around her forehead. The headband matched her tight fitting top and she was wearing blue jeans. They were designer jeans, no doubt. She was gassing up a convertible car, some sort of fancy Volkswagen. She was also wearing sunglasses. She was wearing sunglasses at night. Why? They were white framed and very large, covering nearly half of her face. *Why would someone wear sunglasses at night?* Gary thought hard, as he watched her while pretending to be working his own gas pump. Then it dawned on him, someone who doesn't want to be recognized would wear sunglasses at night. It would have to be someone famous, someone famous with a lot of money! California plates, a convertible, the sunglasses disguise, of course. It was so obvious now. This girl was a famous person. A rich and famous person!

That is when it all began. That is when he realized how easy it could be. How easy it could be to get the money he needed, the money he was *owed*. Gary didn't need to think twice, and he acted fast.

He reached into the cab of his pickup and grabbed his shotgun. He walked right over to the famous blonde girl, who was still looking at her own gas pump. As he got closer behind her, she turned her face toward him. At that moment, he took the shotgun, and lifting it up backward, he brought it down quickly and rapped her in the forehead with the butt stock, hard. She let out a small yelp as her sunglasses flew off her head, and she fell down unconscious right there at the gas pumps.

He had knocked her out cold, just like that. Gary didn't waste any time. With the rifle still in one hand, he scooped her up from the cement. *She is light*, he thought, *maybe only one hundred pounds.* He walked over to his pickup and managed to open the passenger door, and threw the girl in. He then set the shotgun on the seat beside her. He shut the passenger door and ran, as much as a big guy could run anyway, around to the other side and got in. He drove away into the night with his captive. *She could be worth a lot of money,* he thought. *She is probably an actress!* He was very excited at the possibilities. Maybe he could buy the farm. Or he could move to Mexico, or maybe even New Mexico! A whole world was opening up to him. This was turning into a really big deal! As he drove back toward the farm, she started to come to a bit, moaning. He noticed a small trickle of blood running down her face out from under her green headband. As she woke more, he grabbed the Mossberg with one hand and put the barrel to her face. He told her to stay down and keep quiet, which she did.

When he got her back to the farm, he had locked her in his own bedroom closet, telling her if she made a sound, he would kill her. He could hear her sobbing behind the door, but not very loudly.

All he had to do now was wait, wait for the news. Which came the very next day, and it wasn't good. Missing girl from the Baker City, Oregon gas station was Stacie Hathaway, twenty-three years old, and unbelievably, not famous. *Not famous! Why was she wearing sunglasses in the dark?* It made no sense. Gary could not believe it. Was it a trick of some sort? She was just some girl from California passing through on her way to Washington to see her parents? Now what? Maybe he would just let her go. Take her out when it was dark and drop her off. She had seen him though, at the gas station. She had seen his pickup, and this was a small town. Maybe he would just get rid of her, make her missing for good. That would be easier.

He could not make up his mind about it all. He went from being so sure, and so hopeful, to so confused about what to do. He was so mad at himself for his error. He took his half full beer can and threw it across the room at a mangy dog, barely missing it. Beer spilled out all over the dirty wood floor. The skinny dog quickly got up and scurried off to find a hiding spot. The mutt was not about to get its ribs kicked in, again. Gary had no idea what he was going to do now, and he drank most of the day away.

Later came his big break when he watched the six o'clock news. There was a fifty-thousand-dollar reward offered up for any information leading to finding the girl.

Fifty thousand dollars! That was when Gary's plan really took hold. Fifty thousand dollars might not be enough to buy the farm, but it was a lot of money. He didn't need a famous person. He could make a ton money with a bunch of regular people. *Genius!* That is when he decided to make the *apartments.* He would get the farm, or he could even move to New Mexico! *Where's New Mexico anyways?* No matter, he really loved nachos and it sounded nice, real nice, and new. This called for a celebration. *Time to break out the bourbon, Gary old boy!*

14

Dave managed to get himself out of bed and into the shower. The shower felt good; he hadn't slept very well, that was for sure. When finished, he dried himself off in front of the mirror, while staring into his own eyes for no apparent reason. He stood gazing at himself, as if the mirror could somehow give him the answers to his problems, but it didn't.

Then he saw it, right off his left ear, a long white hair sticking straight out sideways, completely horizontal. *How in the world did that happen?* He leaned in to look closer. *How long has that been there?* It was growing right off the edge of his ear. *A long time, I guess.* He felt embarrassed by it. *How many people saw it and didn't say anything?* He pinched it between his fingers, pulled it out, and looked at it. *Must be an inch and a half long! Jessie probably noticed it.* He dropped it to the floor as he leaned forward to look himself over a bit. Satisfied that no other strange anomalies existed, he finished drying off and got dressed.

He grabbed some leftover pizza that he and Jessie ordered in a couple nights before out of the refrigerator, and plopped himself on the couch in front of the TV. He sat staring, not really watching, but lost in his thoughts, the same thoughts he had every long weekend and every long night he spent alone.

He was definitely upset when he and Kat first split, and he was sad for all involved, but mostly for Jessica; she was just thirteen years old at the time. He'd also felt some anger toward Kat for being so stubborn and so impossible to explain things to. Being angry was far better than this self-pity stuff though. Anger at least had direction, outward direction. Anger had an excuse and could always find someone to blame.

The anger wore off though, and for a small time, he felt a sense of hope that he could move on from it all. He was a free man, a bachelor of sorts, that was a good thing, or so they say. It was supposed to be a great time, being single, with endless possibilities. Maybe he was too old for it, or perhaps too boring, but he soon found he just wasn't good at it. He missed his wife and family.

The hope of being free wore off quick; it was a thought that went away as fast as it came. He found himself in his now normal and present state of mind, that of pointless boredom. He was supposed to have "moved on" by now, but he seemed to be actually moving backward, yearning more and more for the past.

Maybe I didn't try hard enough to keep Kat. What killed him most was that his so-called affair really was innocent. He could never convince Kat of it, though. *It would take a miracle for her to ever forgive me.*

What a strange life, was there really any point to it all? Sitting around was depressing, and it was driving him mad. Here he was with all the time in the world to himself, and he couldn't even think of anything to do. He felt as if he was imprisoning or even punishing himself somehow. *The mind is a terrible thing…and mine is getting worse.* He wondered if the airport incident was because of his madness more than anything else. It was hard to imagine him coming home to Kat and Jessie in their happy home saying, *Guess what, I just decked some dude at the airport and shoved a Big Mac down his throat!* That would have been very out of place in his former life, but now, maybe it represented him well.

He decided to get out of the house and go for a drive. He'd check his e-mail and then get out the door to try and blow off some time, maybe swing by the hotel. At least it was somewhere to go for a little while.

Heck, maybe he'd work on the car, not the Focus, though it needed a taillight now, but the Duster. He had an old Plymouth Duster in a storage unit at the apartment complex. He used to tinker with it a lot back at the house and he really liked that car, but he had lost interest in it since Kat left. Why he would lose interest in a hobby when he had nothing better to do, he had no idea.

He walked over to the front window and looked outside. His neighbor from the next-door apartment was out taking care of the flower beds in the complex. Amy was out there helping her, smiling. *Smiling?* The little crippled heroine was out enjoying the day and here he was, sulking. *I have to get out…or I may just go crazy.*

15

Detective Carr's cell phone rang. He was at home with his wife, getting ready to go out and grab some lunch together. He picked up the phone and looked at the caller ID. *Someone from the station…where else?*

He answered. "Hello, this is Matt."

"Hey, Matt, it's Ed, at the station."

"What's up, Ed?"

"We've got something on tape from the airport cameras. A white Ford Focus following the victim's pickup truck up to the third level of the parking garage."

"Ford Focus…Got a plate number?"

"No, the video doesn't have the resolution. We zoomed in but still couldn't make it out. It's definitely a Ford Focus though, going up to the third level at twelve eighteen in the afternoon, then coming back down at twelve twenty-two. It appears to be a white male driving."

Ford Focus…in and out in four minutes. That was quick.

"Oh, a patrol officer also found some pieces of a broken taillight down on level one," Ed added. "The video clip is from a camera on level two, the red Chevy goes by and then the Focus. Then the Focus back the other way. Hard to know for sure if the taillight pieces are from the Focus but—"

"I'm sure they are," Matt interrupted.

Ed agreed, "Yeah."

"Okay, thanks, Ed. This is great info. I appreciate the call."

"Even on a Sunday?" Ed joked

"Not really." Matt laughed. "Take care, buddy."

"You too, Matt. Bye."

"Talk to you later."

He would have to start making some phone calls and try to get John to help out.

For now, however, he was going to go have lunch with his wife. He didn't feel the need to have an emergency right now over that dirtbag lying in the morgue.

16

Kyle zipped up his pants after urinating in the stink hole at the back of the box.

He then picked up the bag of powder by the hole and poured some over the top.

"Not too much," Trip said.

That statement gave Kyle pause. "Not too much" because they could be here a while, and it would not be good to run out of this disinfectant powder stuff, whatever it was. The place already stunk. Trip had been here a week already.

What did this crazy farmer want with them? He didn't want to kill them, it seemed. He could have done that easily by now.

He turned around and Trip was getting a drink from the hose. This farmer guy was feeding them, making sure they had endless water and this makeshift toilet thing. He assumed they were being held for ransom or something. It was the only thing that made sense to him. He wondered where they were.

"Hey, Trip, is that the first time he's shot that gun?"

"Yeah, man, I told you to shut up."

"I know, I know, I'm sorry. It won't happen again. Do you think anyone out there heard that gunshot?"

"I don't know, man. That probably wasn't as loud out there as it was in here."

Kyle grabbed the hose from Trip and took a drink. He quickly closed the small valve at the end, one of those old metal ones like his dad had when he was a kid. "Yeah, probably not," he agreed, then wiped his mouth.

He doubted that the man would shoot at all if he thought someone might hear it. They were probably in the middle of nowhere, either that or nobody in Redneckville paid attention to the sound of a shotgun going off. He had an uncle who lived in Texas that would shoot doves right off his back porch. The neighbors weren't that close but close enough to hear it and nobody cared. It wasn't like hearing a gunshot in the city. It was a perfectly normal sound out in the country. Farmers shot rabbits and coyotes and beer cans all the time.

Kyle studied the box. "We have got to figure a way to get out of here."

"How, man? We can't fit through any of the holes, not even the stinking toilet hole."

"I know, but if we could, you go first," Kyle joked.

Trip smiled, but it didn't last. "What are we going to do, man? We can't get out of this thing."

"I was thinking, maybe we can talk our way out."

"Say what, what do you mean?"

"I don't know," Kyle went on, "maybe we can say one of us is sick, real sick, and get that psycho to open the door and then we take him down."

"Man, you're crazy. That dude doesn't care if we're sick. He—"

Kyle interrupted, "But if one of us was deadly sick, I mean, I think he wants to keep us alive for some reason. We'd be no good to him dead, if so, he would have killed us already."

"So we'll just say I'm sick, and he's going to open up the door all ready to take me to the doctor? Oh, hey, Doc, this is my black son. Oh, you don't remember him? Well, he's sick," Trip said sarcastically.

"Well I could be the sick one."

"Honestly, dude, I don't think the dude really cares if we're sick."

"Yeah, I know, it's stupid. I guess not," Kyle said quietly. "But we gotta think of something though. I can't just sit here like this."

"I dunno, man. This dude has us locked up pretty tight."

Kyle was still thinking. "What if we hid from him, like made him think we weren't in here anymore. I bet he would open the door then."

"Where are we gonna hide, man? Where are we gonna hide in here?"

"I don't know. I'm just trying to think outside the box here."

"Real funny," Trip said.

"What? What's funny?" Kyle said, then it dawned on him. "Oh, man…"

They both laughed, as much as their situation allowed, at the remark, as dumb as it was.

Kyle looked around the container. Maybe there were places they could get down into a corner where the man wouldn't be able to see them from the outside. There were also blankets they could use to hide under. If they stayed really quiet, maybe he would open the door. Maybe he would open the door and come inside, and they could jump up and take off running. If they were fast enough, they could shut the door behind them and lock the man in the box!

The more he thought about it, the more he liked the idea. He was big man though, with a gun, no less. Didn't he put his gun down somewhere though? When he shot the gun into the box, it seemed like he walked over and picked it up from somewhere first. He must have set it down when he dropped the bread through the slat. If they couldn't shut the door on him, what if they could get their hands on that gun? He ran through his mind how to pump a shotgun. He had done some pheasant hunting with his dad a couple years ago. Operating a shotgun was about as easy as it gets. Pump it and pull the trigger.

He thought about the safety. It could be on top and operated with your thumb. He made the motion of pushing an imaginary safety off with his thumb. Or it could be down in the trigger guard, where you would push it with your finger. Thanks to his dad, Kyle knew his way around guns okay. He hoped it would pay off.

He pictured the big bad man begging for his life, as he pointed the gun at his chest. If he made a move, he would blast a giant hole right through that psycho. He swore he would. That would be awesome.

17

2:00 PM

Jessica's cell phone rang. She looked at the screen. It was an Idaho number, but she didn't recognize it. Maybe it was one of her friends.

"Hello?"

"Yes, hello, is this Jessica Preston?"

It was a man's voice. Her heart sped up a bit; it was an adult, a stranger.

"Um, yes."

"Oh, hi, Jessica, I'm sorry to bother you. My name is Matthew Carr, and I'm a police officer in Boise Idaho. I'm calling about an incident that happened at the Boise airport."

Jessica felt her heart beat a bit harder.

"Um…okay," she said.

Sensing her nervousness and reminding himself that the girl was young, Carr said, "Everything is fine. There was hit-and-run accident, and we're just looking for anyone who may have seen it happen, so we're just calling people that were at the airport at the time of the accident, hoping to find a lead."

That's kind of cool, Jessica thought, but she couldn't help.

"Oh, okay. I didn't see anything happen."

"Okay…What time were you at the airport? Do you remember?" Carr asked

"Around eleven thirty."

"How did you get there?"

"My dad dropped me off."

"What does he drive?"

"A, um…" She forgot what kind of car it was. *Duh.* She suddenly remembered. "Oh, it's a Ford Focus."

"Oh." *This is good*, Carr thought. *Should I push it? Yes.* "What color?"

"Um…white, but we didn't get in a crash."

"Oh…Okay…but did your dad mention seeing an accident?"

"No."

"Have you talked to him recently?"

"No, not since coming home. I mean, no, I haven't."

"Coming home? You don't live in Idaho?"

"Well I do, but um, well Mom is here now and my dad is in Idaho."

There was a pause, Carr thought quickly and said, "Oh, okay. Did your dad just drop you off or did he park at the airport?"

"He parked."

"In the short-term lot I would assume?"

"Yes." *This is kind of a strange conversation*, Jessica thought. She wondered if it was some kind of phone scam thing or something.

"Oh well, okay. Hmmm…Well, I guess that's it then." He acted as if this was just another dead-end, then he added, "Do you think it would be okay to call your dad, in case he saw something?"

"Yeah, sure…I mean, I guess."

"What's his name?"

"Dave."

"Dave…David Preston? Same last name?"

"Yes," she said, but she felt strange for giving out the information. Maybe she should just hang up now, but the man didn't sound like a scammer or anything. He actually sounded really nice.

"Well, thanks so much, Jessica. I guess I'll just keep going down my list of people to call, hopefully somebody saw *something*," he said lightly, trying to reassure her all was okay. "Bye now, and thank you for your time. I do appreciate it."

"Okay, bye." *That was weird*, Jessica thought. She was happy to be off the phone, which was rare for a fourteen-year-old girl.

Bingo! David Preston. Detective Carr had found his suspect after only forty or so calls. *This was too easy—for once.*

18

Dave didn't make it out the front door after all. He continued to lie on the couch, paralyzed in front of the TV. Some English soccer game was on, but he wasn't paying much attention. Jessie was a soccer player, and they used to watch these kinds of games together and it was a lot of fun. Now however, watching alone was boring.

He ran through his head of what he would say to Jessie about his so-called affair when he got the nerve to call her. His mind wandered back to when Kathy caught him with the "other" woman—the day when Kathy was betrayed by the man she loved.

Tina-Rae was her name, not Tina, but Tina-Rae. As her name might suggest, she was from Texas, Houston in fact. She came into the hotel late one night while he was working the front desk. She seemed very friendly, but not flirtatious. She had that Texas southern accent, which was charming as all get out and sure went well with her wide white smile. She was pretty, no doubt; she had long brown hair, pulled back from her full face, tan skin, and dark-blue eyes. She was in her late thirties, but still looked great. Not a knockout, though she surely was when she was twenty years old and twenty pounds lighter. She probably was a little less attractive without her makeup, of course, but she wore it well. Dave imagined she was likely a cheerleader in high school and probably even in some big Texas university.

He didn't think too much of her when she first checked in. He just checked her in like any other guest and forgot about it. She returned though, every couple of months or so on business, and after a while, they just sort of became friends. Not friends like the kind you call and talk to on the weekend, but familiar faces. It was the sort of relationship you might have with the guy who always fixes your car and calls you by your first name.

One night, Tina-Rae asked him if he would like to grab some dinner with her. It was so off the cuff and casual that without thinking, he said, "Sure." He left the hotel with an assistant manager, and he and Tina-Rae went out to the local Chili's for a bite to eat, just friends, talking and eating together.

He liked her. She didn't talk about business, like most self-important business travelers did. She talked about her family, her kids, her husband, all that sort of stuff. The whole evening together lasted an hour, tops. He even thought about telling Kathy about it, but never did. He didn't see any reason to get some big thing started when there was no big thing going on. He figured some cans of worms are better left unopened.

The dinners with Tina-Rae soon became a regular thing when she was in town. He had to admit it. He was quite fond of her. He knew the feeling was mutual, but they both were married and wanted to keep it that way, so the relationship stayed as it was—friends.

That is, until he came home one night after eating out with Tina-Rae and as soon as he walked in his door, Kathy drilled him about *who this woman was he had been seeing.*

"Who is she?" she yelled at him, right when he walked through the door. No "Hello," no "How was work?" None of that.

Shocked, he responded, "Who? What are you talking about?"

"The woman you were having dinner with last night, who is she?"

How could she possibly know that? "I have no idea what you're talking about," he lied.

"You were eating dinner with a woman! Beth saw you! She saw you, David! Who is she?" She was very upset, calling him by his whole name, crying and shaking, her makeup running all around her eyes. He felt the blood drain from his face. *This is not good. Thanks a million, Beth!*

Beth was Kathy's friend from church. He didn't see her at the restaurant, but she apparently saw him, that much was evident.

"Kathy, settle down—" As soon as he said it, he knew his mistake in choice of words. Never tell a woman to settle down, at least not Kat.

"Settle down?" she yelled.

"Okay, okay, honey, hold on, it's okay. Let me explain."

"So it *was* you!" she yelled. "Oh, David…" She started sobbing, almost uncontrollably.

Wow, he thought. *This woman is borderline crazy right now, starting to get out of hand. I better think. Would the truth work here? I doubt it.* He felt terrible about it, but he lied again, "Kat, listen, I was at dinner but it was with a group of people, not with just one woman."

She was still crying and trying to speak, "Beth saw you, David! Just you and a woman at the Willow Creek Grille. Beth saw you!"

He thought about where they were sitting in that restaurant. *Was it a table for two? No.* They were in a booth that could easily fit four people.

He continued his lie, "Honey, there were four people eating. They're from some banking firm. They stay at the hotel all the time. They just invited me out for dinner, that's all. They come into town all the time. They know me just from staying at the hotel every month or so. It's no big deal, I promise."

She looked him straight in the eye, trying hard to become a human lie detector. "Beth said it was you and a woman, that's it." She stared at him intently, waiting.

He stared back. "Then she's crazy. It was a group of people, Kat." His voice did not waver. He felt sick. He was hoping it didn't show, but having gotten on this road, he was going to have to stick to it.

He could strangle that stupid Beth woman. She was always a nosy one, gossiping about everyone, like it was some sort of badge of honor to get into everyone's business. It might be understandable if Beth was truly concerned about Kathy, but he doubted it. Even Kathy hated Beth's gossiping. She even gossiped about Beth's gossiping. In this case however, she wasn't going to let it go away as easily as. "Well, we all know how Beth is."

Though it seemed humanly impossible, Kat raised her voice even more. "Then why did you lie when I first asked you about it? Why did you deny it? Tell me that, David! Why!"

Man, she was angry.

Again, she yelled through her tears, "Why did you lie, David? Why did you lie to me?"

Because I didn't want this to happen, that's why, he thought. He was being accused of cheating, which simply was not the case. Even though he was guilty, sort of, he just couldn't change his course. He figured, at this point, coming clean would ruin their marriage forever. How could he suddenly say his side of the story was a complete lie after all of this? He could, but he just couldn't.

Holding his ground, he looked at her again. "Well gee, maybe it's because when I walked in the door, you jumped down my throat about seeing some woman. I've never cheated on you Kat, and I never will, ever."

The conversation went on and on like this for hours. Dave finally convinced her that Beth must have seen him with Tina-Rae while the other two, both men, by the way, were at the bar getting drinks for everyone. He apologized profusely, over and over again. He told Kathy how much he loved her. He even suggested that they call Beth, even though he knew Kat wouldn't do that. Was Kathy really convinced by his lies, or was she just exhausted?

He couldn't imagine how long Beth could have been studying them, or what she actually saw. That restaurant is a pretty small place. It seems he would have seen her if she was in there. They ate dinner pretty late that night; his best guess was that Beth was on her way out when she saw him with Tina-Rae.

Anyway, he got through the night, and they never spoke another word about it.

From that day, things between them changed. He knew in his heart he was a liar. He had lied to the person he swore before God and to a church full of people that he would never lie to. He had lied to the love of his life, his wife.

He wasn't sure if Kat really believed him or not; things were tense. After a few weeks, it seemed as if Kathy had just checked out. He of course was on his best behavior, but it seemed Kat really didn't care. The trust was gone, and it showed in her face. He had literally stolen the sparkle from her eyes, and it was replaced with a haze. She was merely tolerating him. She loved him, but no longer could trust him, and it showed in her expression and in her interactions with him. Their lives became less about their relationship and more about the logistics of daily life. They were like roommates.

As the months went by, it seemed to get better, but "better" didn't last very long.

He was working the front desk one afternoon when who comes strolling in with her big smile but Tina-Rae. The hotel is very quiet at that time of day. He stepped around the desk and told Tina-Rae he needed to talk to her. He knew it was just a matter of time, and he knew what he had to do; he had to tell her he couldn't see her anymore. It was like he was breaking up with her, which sounded ridiculous, but was exactly what it felt like.

He told her the whole story about what had happened between him and Kathy. Tina-Rae felt terrible and guilty for how she was involved in it all. He assured her it was okay, that she hadn't ruined his marriage, and things would be fine between him and Kat. She decided she would find a different place to stay going forward, and he agreed that would probably be best.

She reached her arms out to give him a hug, and he stepped toward her, closed his eyes and hugged her deep and hard. It was the first time he had ever even touched her.

She smelled nice, and admittedly, she felt nice; he knew he was hugging her longer that he should be, but he didn't care.

He finally let up and slowly opened his eyes to see Kathy and Jessica standing before him, just inside the hotel's front door! Kat's eyes burned right through him. He had never seen a look on her face like that before. She quickly grabbed Jessica's hand and turned, hurrying out the door toward the parking lot.

He gasped in shock and stood motionless, trying to compute what had just happened. He let go of Tina-Rae, flew to the door, threw it open and ran out calling. "Kathy, wait...wait!"

"Get in the car, Jessie!" Kathy yelled.

Jessica ran around the other side and got in the car. Kathy got in and slammed her door shut. He ran to the car, putting his hands on the door glass. He saw tears streaming down her face. He pleaded, "Wait! Kathy, stop! Wait!" She didn't even look at him. She just quickly started the car up and sped away as he jumped back to avoid getting his feet run over.

Jessica looked back at him through the back window, an image he would not soon forget.

He stood alone in the parking lot, a lifeless fool, or maybe *tool* was a better word for it.

That was it. He called in a different manager, gave not so much a nod to Tina-Rae, who stood dumbfounded in the hotel lobby, and raced home to tell the truth, the whole truth, and nothing but the truth.

It was too late. It was more than Kat could take. She didn't know what to believe about him anymore. She and Jessica left him—alone.

Now his mind weighed on having to relive the whole thing again as he told Jessica the story. She needed to know though. It was the right thing to do.

19

4:00 PM

Detective Carr pulled up to the Preston residence and parked out in front. A squad car followed and parked behind him. The two cops exited their vehicles. Matt fished out some gum from his pocket.

It was a nice upper-middle-class neighborhood, clean and quiet, except for the noise of a lawnmower coming from behind the house. The front lawn was freshly mowed, and the gate to a wooden fence was opened up to the backyard. *Was their suspect casually mowing his lawn?*

The two men went up to the front door and knocked hard—no answer. They looked at each other and headed toward the open gate leading to the backyard. They walked around the side of the house, and there was a man mowing the back lawn coming right toward them. The man looked to be in his sixties and in decent shape for his age. He saw them instantly, shut off the mower, and, as it wound down, walked toward the officers. "Can I help you?" he asked

Carr extended his hand and said, "I'm Detective Matthew Carr, and this here is Officer Grant Brayley. We're with the Boise PD."

The man shook Carr's hand and nodded to the uniformed officer. "Kellan Rainey. Nice to meet you."

Matt continued, "We are here to see Dave Preston. This is his residence, correct?"

"Yes, sir, but you won't find him here."

"Why is that?" Carr asked

"He moved out a few months back. He and his wife separated. Too bad…really nice people. They have a daughter. Hate to see that happen, you know. Seems like no one stays together anymore."

"And you are a relative?"

"Neighbor, right there," the man pointed to his house next door. "Kathy went to Denver, and I'm just keeping the place up for her while she's gone."

"Kathy? The wife, yes?"

"Yes, sir. If you don't mind me asking, what is all this about anyway?"

No one ever seems to mind asking. "Oh…Mr. Preston was possibly witness to a hit-and-run accident and we just need to talk to him. We're just seeing if he can help us out a bit. Do you know where he's living at the moment?"

The man looked at the sky, as if that was somehow going to help him answer the question more accurately. "Let's see…all I know is he moved into an apartment in downtown Boise. Don't really know where though. Hit-and-run, huh? Someone get killed?"

Damn! He ignored the last question about the hit-and-run. "Anyone around that might know where he lives? It's pretty important we talk to him today."

The man stared off to the sky again thinking. "None that I can think of."

They were getting nowhere with this guy. They thanked him for his time and headed back toward the cars parked on the street. "Dead-end," Matt said to Officer Brayley. "I'm good from here. Thanks for coming along."

"No problem. Good luck, sir."

Matt got in his car and called Detective Weatherford. He answered after the first ring. "What's up, Matt?"

"Need a favor, John. Could you pull up everything you can on Dave Preston? This is related to the airport incident."

"Got it. Will do."

"Thanks," Matt said and hung up.

20

It was nearly dinnertime when Dave finally decided to get out of his apartment. He felt like a fool for doing absolutely nothing but sulk all day long. That has become his way though; no matter how many times he told himself he would snap out of it, he just couldn't. Always the same result, a struggle between who he was now and who he wished to be, a husband and a father.

He went out, grabbed a quick bite, and decided he would stop by the hotel and at least have some human contact today. Zach would be working the front counter tonight, and he was always lively and positive. It might do him some good to see Zach. It would take his mind off things, at least temporarily.

Zach was an ex-Boise State football player, a defensive lineman. Dave had hired him himself. He was an intelligent, twenty-something gentle giant, who had come in quite handy as a bouncer on occasion. With his presence, he could clear out a teenage party room just by asking nicely.

"Hey, boss," Zach said, as Dave walked through the front door into the lobby. "How's it going?"

"Good," Dave said. "Just thought I'd swing by and see how things are going here."

"Pretty quiet I'd say. Just trying to stay awake," he joked. "What are you up to tonight?"

"Honestly," Dave admitted, "not a damn thing."

"Not likely to find much excitement here, boss."

"Please don't call me that," Dave said, knowing Zach was messing with him.

"What?" Zach joked again. "But you love being called that, remember?"

"Oh yeah, I do remember now, employee," Dave joked back.

Zach laughed. "*Employee*, huh? Does have a certain ring to it."

Then Zach's eyes suddenly lit up. "Oh, hey, did you hear about the cheeseburger killer?"

"Huh?"

What did he just say?

"Yeah, they found this guy dead at the airport with a cheeseburger jammed in his..." Zach's voice trailed off as he noticed a change in his boss's complexion.

Dave's throat closed up, his face got hot, and his head swooned. As casually as he possibly could, he bent down, pretending to tie his shoe.

Zach's voice continued, "So yeah, apparently they haven't found the killer yet. Pretty crazy, eh? A cheeseburger jammed right down..."

Dave, still down on his knee, said quietly, "Yeah, uh, that is crazy." *Did my voice crack?* He felt cold sweat drip from his right armpit and run down his side. His head was blazing hot.

He slowly got up and said, "I need to use the bathroom." He quickly walked away from Zach toward the restroom down the hallway.

"Hey, you okay?" Zach called out to him.

"Fine, yeah, maybe something I ate. I don't know..." Dave said without turning back. He felt like his legs were going to collapse, but he kept moving. *My lips feel tight. Just keep walking,* he told himself. *Do not fall over. Keep going.*

Dave made it into the bathroom, and thankfully, it was empty. His heart was pounding in his chest. *Killer...dead man...airport...cheeseburger killer? Me? Cheeseburger killer?*

The image of him shoving that cheeseburger into that guy's mouth flashed across his mind. *My God! Am I the cheeseburger killer? I am!*

The bathroom suddenly felt like a dungeon closing in on him; he was sure he was going to pass out. Through his tunnel vision, he was able to exit the bathroom door, run down to the end of the hallway, and shove open the door into the stairwell. He ran up the stairs, digging his wallet out of his back pocket, pulling the master key card out of the wallet as he burst through the door going to the third floor.

Room 327, being next to a giant AC unit at the stairwell, was one of the noisiest rooms in the hotel. The room was never rented out, unless they were completely full. Everyone complained about the noise. Dave knew it would be vacant. He slid his key in the door slot, opened the door, went in, shut the door behind him, and stood there frozen, not knowing what to do next.

Throw up. That's what I have to do.

He ran to the bathroom lifted the toilet lid, bent over, and wretched trying to puke it all out. *Clean it all out... every sin...every lie...everything!*

He convulsed and sweated but produced nothing. He leaned with his hands on his knees over the toilet shaking. He tried to stick his finger down his throat to make something happen, but it only caused gagging and watery eyes.

21

Detective Carr was not happy. *Cheeseburger killer? Who in the hell talked to the press about this besides me!*

He'd never mentioned anything about the possibility of a second person involved in the death of the man at the airport. He certainly didn't give any details about the cheeseburger.

The cat's out of the bag now. Looks like it is going to be a long Sunday after all.

22

Dave snapped himself out of a trance in the bathroom, went into the bedroom, and turned on the TV. He flipped through to the guide channel to see if any local news was on, but he knew at this time there wouldn't be. His mind was racing; he had to see this news story. As he suspected, there was nothing on but sitcom reruns and sports.

Computer in the lobby! I can get on the computer in the lobby and look it up online! Zach was down there, though. He didn't want anyone to see him in this condition; he still felt as if he could pass out at any second.

Am I breathing? Yes. Good…deep breath…think…think… think! Laptop in the car? Yes, it's in the car. Good…go…hurry! He opened the room door slowly and looked out both ways. A couple of kids in swimsuits were way down the hallway and were waiting for the elevator. That was it.

He turned in the opposite direction, into the stairwell, ran down the stairs, out the side door to his car, got in, looked out the window, and slumped down in his seat. He reached in the backseat, ripped the laptop out of its case, and hit the power-on button.

It seemed to be taking forever! *C'mon. C'mon, you slow piece of crap. Boot up!* Finally, he was able to open up an internet browser and connect to the hotel's Wi-Fi system. He went to the local news channel website.

There it is! To his horror, it was right on the front page! "Cheeseburger Killer Strikes at Airport!" *Strikes?* He glanced around the parking lot again and began reading the story. It was short.

He couldn't believe it; he read over it three times. The man was dead. He was from California. Police have no suspect in the case at this time. No suspect, that was good, he guessed. *If you have any information, please call. No suspect. Yes, that's good, right?*

Cheeseburger killer. Unbelievable. His hands were shaking, more sweat ran down his side from his armpit. He thought he heard a siren and nearly jumped out of his skin. *Is it the cops?* Then it rang out again, and he twitched in his seat toward the sound. It was his cell phone. *Man, am I on edge!* He tried to calm himself and picked up the phone off the passenger seat. It was Jessica. *What does she want?* He took a deep breath and answered, "Hi, Jessie," trying to sound cheerful and as normal as possible.

"Hi, Dad, what's up?"

He really didn't feel like small talk just now, that was for sure. "I'm at work, sweetie. What do you need?"

"Oh, I'm sorry, Dad. On a Sunday?"

"Yeah, I got called in," he lied.

"Oh well, I just wanted to tell you that some cop called and"—Again, his head swooned and his forehead became hot. He closed his eyes and tried to listen closely to what she was saying. *This isn't small talk after all*—"he was wondering where you live."

Dave turned his mouth from the phone and took a big deep breath. "Why? What did he want?" he asked, still feigning normalcy. "He wanted to talk to you about an accident at the airport."

Dave was getting tunnel vision again. *Deep breath. What accident? The cheeseburger accident?* "What accident?"

"A hit-and-run at the airport. They thought maybe you saw it and wanted to talk to you about it."

Hit-and-run. What's she talking about? He tried to think. *Hit-and-run?* It did seem vaguely familiar. He couldn't think. Was he pausing too long with Jessica on the other end? Why did he feel he should know about this. *Hit-and-run?* He hummed into the phone to show Jessica he was thinking, not frozen like he was in reality. *Hit-and-run. Hit-and-run? The S-10. That hit-and-run! Oh man, they know all about it. They know. They have a suspect now and it's me!*

"Dad?"

Deep breaths. "Yeah, I'm here, just thinking…um, so… uh…What did you say to him? This…guy, the cop guy."

"Um…well, he wanted to talk to you, so I gave him your number"—*WHAT! Breathe…easy…nice and easy*— "because I don't really know where your apartment is. I didn't really pay attention."

Dave opened his eyes wide. *What did she just say?* He needed to calm down so he could get this info. He knew that, so he got himself together as best he could. It was important. "You said you gave him my number because you don't know where I live?

"Yeah."

Short answer…not enough. "So…" Dave said, trying to remain calm, "he asked where I live?"

"Yeah, but I don't really know your address. Sorry."

"Okay, so you gave him my number." He was trying very hard not to sound irritated.

"Uh…yeah, because he wanted to talk to you about the accident and stuff."

"Please don't give my number out, honey. It may not even be a real cop." Trying not be harsh, he added, "Could be a salesman. They do crap like that to kids to get numbers."

"Oh! Sorry, Dad, I know, but I think he was a real cop, I think. Sorry. He called again yesterday too."

"What?"

"He called yesterday after I got home, wondering if we saw a hit-and-run accident. It was kinda weird."

"What did he say?"

"He wondered if we saw it, and I said no, so he wondered if maybe you saw it, and I said I don't know."

"Yesterday?"

"Yeah."

Why would he call again?

"Why did he call back then? Did he say anything?"

"I dunno…I guess to get your number, so he could call you."

"He didn't ask for my number the first time?"

"Um, no, I don't think so. No, I guess not."

Dave was putting all the info together. He suddenly felt the urge to get out of the hotel parking lot. He had to end this phone call and get moving. Suddenly, getting out of there became the only thing he could think about. *I've gotta go.*

"Sorry for giving out your number, Dad. I really didn't—

He interrupted, "No, no, it's okay. I'll talk to him if he calls, no problem, sweetheart. I better get going. Love you. If he calls you again, let me know, okay? Love you."

"Okay. Love you too, Dad. Um, Dad, one more thing…"

Oh no! What could this be?

"Um…Dad, I wanted to tell you that…um…well…I believe you. You know, about that girl and all."

What's she talking about now? "What do you mean, Jessie? What girl?"

"That lady…you know." He could tell she was nervous. "Um…you know…I believe you about her…that she was just a friend and all…and um, I heard you and Mom talking that night and you know, when that happened and well…I believe you. I just wanted to tell you."

She was breaking his heart. *She heard us arguing all night? Oh man.* "Jessica…" he said softly, "thank you, I love you, and, yes, she was just a friend, but I did lie to your mom. I think you should know that."

"Um…Yeah, I know, but I mean…I believe you that… you know…um…never kissed her or whatever."

Poor kid…of all the bad timing. Dave felt terrible, but he still had an urgency to get moving. "Jessie, thank you, I love you, and you're right, I never did and never would, but I really gotta get going. We can talk later about it if you like."

"Um, no, that's okay. I just wanted to tell you that, and um…also…I think Mom believes you too, but she's just… Well, she is still pretty mad, I guess."

"I know, sweetie. It's okay. I'll talk to you soon, okay?"

"Okay, bye, Dad, love you."

"Love you too, angel," he said and hung up.

I really need to get moving here! He threw the phone and the laptop on the passenger seat, dug the keys out of his front pocket, fired up the car, and got the hell out of there.

23

Gary walked in his house back from the grocery store where he picked up some more bread, beer, dog food, and some paper. The dog watched as he walked in but kept her distance. Gary threw everything on the kitchen table except for the dog food. He ripped the top off of the 20-lb dog food bag off as he walked to the living room area and dropped it on the floor. Dog food spilled out on the floor as the bag fell over. As Gary turned to go back to the kitchen, the dog moved in and started eating, as though it hadn't eaten in a week, which it hadn't.

Gary went to the fridge, grabbed a beer, and opened it. He pulled open a kitchen drawer with a large dirty hand and grabbed a pen. He was ready to start making some serious money, and he was serious about it too.

He sat down at the kitchen table to write his note on the brand new paper he just bought. He opened up the paper package and pulled out a few sheets. He wasn't much good for writing, but he wanted it to sound really official.

HERE LIES

He stopped, here lies who? Which one would be first? He couldn't remember the kids' names at the moment. What was it? Kyle. That was it. He went on.

HERE LIES KYLE. THARE ARE OTHERS

Here lies Kyle? That would mean he is dead, right? Gary was suddenly getting confused. He wanted the money, but would people pay for dead kids? Maybe they would, but he wasn't so sure. They would pay to get alive kids back though, but he also had to be taken seriously. He could just kill one kid and then ask more money for the others. Perfect. It was pure genius. He really figured that out fast. He wasn't confused anymore. *That Albert Einwise guy didn't have anything on Gary the genius. Einwise probably wasn't even his real name. Bet he made it up just to sound smart. What did that stupid nerd do anyway? Invent glasses or something? Who cares? How much money did I need?* He remembered once someone at the store telling him the farm was worth almost a million dollars.

He wanted a lot more than that. *Let's see. There was a million, a billion, and a zillion. A billion? Was that a lot? Was it more than a million? A, B, C, D. B came before the* M *in million, so a billion was less than a million. Z was the last letter so a zillion was the most money ever.* That was a lot to ask for. That was maybe all the money in the world. He figured they would probably try to talk him down if he asked for a zillion, which was at the end of the alphabet. They might try to come down into the middle somewhere. Like a million or maybe a jillion. If he asked for a million, they would probably try to take him all the way back to *B*, which was only a billion. *He better go for the zillion and no trades!*

He continued his letter.

> HERE LIES KYLE. THARE OTHERS THAT ARE STILL A LIVE. BUT THEY CULD BE DEAD SOON BUT NOT IF I GITS MY MONEY. A ZILLON DOLLORS. I WILL CALL THE COPS TO SAY WHARE TO PUTS THE MONEY IFS I DONT GITS AWAY OR SOMES FOLLOW ME MY FRENS WILL SHOOT THEM AND YOU AND THEY ALL WILL DIE.

He read it over. It looked really good. He lied about having friends that could shoot, so he made them up. He felt sort of bad about lying but that was okay. Dad wasn't here to whoop on him anymore for lying. Dad wasn't around for anything anymore. He bet his brother would be proud of him. When Gary killed his dad, his older brother brought him out here, told him to find work, and never, ever, ever come back home. Gary's brother didn't seem all that mad that Gary killed their dad, but he didn't want Gary to jail for it either. That was a long time ago. Gary hadn't seen his brother since. Gary knew his brother would be proud of him now. He was going to be rich and famous!

He stood up with a big smile on his face, a big yellowish-brown grin. That grin faded instantly though when he caught his knee on the table and his beer toppled over, spilling across his wonderful note. The ink smeared and it was all wet and looked terrible. He picked up the soggy note. You couldn't read it anymore!

He banged his fist on the table, and the dog ran off to go hide somewhere. He looked at the note again. It was ruined! He picked it up off the table and threw it at the wall. Growing even more angry, Gary tossed the table over against the kitchen wall. He cursed and stomped around the kitchen like a child having a hissy fit. Looking for something to take his anger out on, he snatched up a dirty dish out of the sink and smashed it on the counter. He stood there clenching his fists, shaking with rage, his vision blurring.

After a few moments of huffing and puffing, he walked back over by the table, casually kicked some beer cans and other dirty dishes out of the way, and picked up his pen. He also grabbed the table off the floor and slammed it down upright on its four legs. Gary then got himself another piece of paper to start all over again. He was still fuming. A note that good was going to be really hard to do all over again!

24

Detective Carr picked up his phone and looked at who was calling. It was Weatherford. He answered, "Hey, John, whatchya got?"

"All the info I could round up on Dave Preston. Seems he's pretty squeaky clean. Besides a couple minor traffic violations, he's got no criminal record at all."

That's probably all going to change really soon. "What else?"

John read off a cell number matching the one Preston's daughter had already provided, the address of his apartment, and that of his workplace, the Marriott downtown.

Well, time to go round up our man.

He wouldn't risk spooking him with a phone call. He would send someone to the hotel while he and John checked the apartment. That's where he figured they would find him.

Hope he hasn't seen that cheeseburger killer BS that was on the news earlier. I hope...

25

Dave drove past his apartment building, all looked normal. *No cops.*

Was there anything he really needed in his apartment? Clothes would be about it. He didn't really *need* clothes though. Surely, grabbing some clothes wouldn't be worth risking going to prison. He headed on down the road another couple miles to the Super Stor-it storage place. He rented a storage garage there when he moved out of the house.

He punched in his secret code on a little pad outside the gate and drove inside as the gate slowly swung open. He drove down in between the rows of storage garages, then parked just past his own space. He got out, turned the tumblers on the combination lock to Jessica's birth date, and lifted the door.

He had some boxes and stuff on top of it, but he cleared them off quickly, revealing his Plymouth Duster. It was once his father's car, but his dad handed it down to him some fifteen years ago before he passed away. He remembered driving around in it with his dad when he was a kid; even back then, everyone loved this car. It was bright orange, or Vitamin C as Chrysler Corporation called it. It wasn't exactly a low-profile car, but it wasn't a white Ford Focus either, so it would have to do. He imagined himself outrunning the cops in this car, sirens wailing, blue lights blazing, and him speeding toward the state line at full throttle, making his great getaway to freedom.

He climbed in, prayed the engine would fire up, and turned the key. The starter spun and whined, working hard to turn the motor over and over and over, but no ignition occurred.

It's okay. This is how it is after the car has sat for a while. The fuel pump just needs to get fuel pushed up to the carb and then it will fire. It has to.

He cranked again; the motor turned and turned, the starter whirred and whined, drawing every amp it could from the battery. Dave pictured the fuel line filling up and filling up the carburetor.

Just when the battery had nearly drained completely, the motor sparked to life with a roar; it was likely the most beautiful sound he ever heard. He put his foot in it slightly to warm it up and keep it running. It blew out a good amount of smoke initially but quickly cleared up. He kept the motor revved up for a few seconds and then let off to make sure it would idle on it's own. It idled a little rough, but it was good to go. It sounded great; if his mind wasn't on more important things, he would be smiling from ear to ear at the sound of the exhaust note.

He pulled the Duster out of the storage garage, got out, and did a quick look-around for anything else he might need.

Toolbox…Weed eater…furniture…mostly just a bunch of junk in here…I should have just thrown it all out. There was a small suitcase though, on the floor behind where the car had been. He couldn't remember what was in it, if anything. He grabbed it. It had something in it all right, probably clothes. He flipped it over and opened it up. *Yes, just some old clothes. Why do I even keep this stuff?* Then he remembered something else.

He dug his hands through the clothes to rediscover yet another incredible gift from his father, an old Colt 45 handgun. He looked at it intently, trying to remember what his father had taught him about it. He wasn't completely familiar with guns, but it wasn't exactly rocket science. He dropped the magazine out, saw it was loaded, then pulled back the slide, and looked in the chamber. *Empty...okay, good...simple.* He let the slide forward and slid the magazine back in the grip. Then he put the gun back down into the suitcase. *Should I bring it with me?* He could probably use the suitcase with the old clothes, even though they smelled a bit musty. He couldn't risk going back to his apartment and didn't want to be hanging around here for very long either.

He quickly looked in some of the other boxes—nothing really—papers, magazines, and books. *All junk.* He had no idea why he bothered even storing this crap, but he had no time for that now.

He zipped up the suitcase, gun and all, jogged out to the Duster, threw it in the back, climbed in the Focus, and pulled it into the garage. He was ready to roll on out of there when it occurred to him that the Duster didn't have recent tags. That would have been a major oversight. The last thing he wanted to do was to get pulled over for an expired registration. *I could pull the plates off the Focus and put them on the Duster.*

He quickly grabbed a screwdriver out of the toolbox, took the plates from the Focus and swapped them on for the expired ones on his getaway car. The plates wouldn't match the car if they ran the numbers, but at least they would look legitimate.

He pulled the garage door shut and locked it down, jumped in his Detroit iron horse, and hit the road. He was scared as hell, but one thing he knew for sure, prison was no place for someone like himself. Besides, he didn't mean to kill the guy. That wasn't his intent at all, but intent likely didn't matter. Prison was not in his future. He wasn't sure what was.

It was time to get out of Dodge, in his Plymouth. He soon found his way to the freeway and started heading east.

26

Detective Carr knocked and knocked on Dave Preston's apartment door, but it was apparent that he wasn't there. The white Ford Focus was nowhere to be found in the area either.

It was the same story at the hotel. Preston had been there just a couple hours earlier. The big kid at the desk thought maybe he got sick and went home. *Apparently not. Where is he? Is he on the run? Damn!* He had hoped to find him face-to-face. Now he was going to have to call him. People can do weird things when cops call them. They can become very irrational. He picked up his phone and dialed Mr. Preston's cell number.

27

Dave had moved along pretty well and was gassing up the Plymouth at a truck stop outside Twin Falls, Idaho, when he heard his phone ringing on the seat. Keeping his head down, he ducked into the car to look at the number. He didn't recognize it, and he didn't answer it either. Then something dawned on him. Actually, it hit him like a bolt of lightning. *The phone! They can track you with those things, but only if you answer it, right?* Could they triangulate or GPS his location just by calling him even if he didn't answer? He wasn't sure, so he just turned it off completely.

He finished filling the tank and headed into the store to get a few things.

Sitting on the sidewalk by the store entrance was a burned-out-looking lanky guy drinking something hidden by a brown paper bag. He had dirty jeans on and an equally dirty baby-blue puffy vest with no shirt on underneath. He was wearing a camouflage ball cap with the bill curved and pulled low over his eyes. He was probably a transient dropped off here by a trucker that couldn't take the smell or conversation anymore. Dave walked by him, trying not to make eye contact, but of course, the man spoke up.

"Nice-looking car ya got there, brother."

Dave quickly said, without looking, "Um…oh, yeah… thanks," and kept walking past the man, toward the door.

"It gots a 340 in it, does it?"

Did the giant "340" decal on the side give it away?

"Um…yep," Dave answered as he entered the store.

Can't anyone just mind their own business anymore?

He was thinking now that maybe he should have locked the car. He watched the man for a moment through the store window. The guy just sat there drinking his *whatever*, so Dave got on with his shopping.

It was a pretty good-sized store actually. It didn't look like much from the outside, but it had a little bit of everything. It even had a small restaurant connected at one end. It smelled like fried fish. One one side of the store was an automotive and T-shirt section. There were shirts with all kinds of stupid slogans on them that only a doped up teenager, or a moron would actually find amusing. It seemed an insult to truckers that you could only find such garbage at a truck stop or a Walmart.

There was southwestern-style jewelry section of mostly turquoise and silver pieces. Next to that was a large glass display case full of pocketknives and stun guns, swords, throwing stars, and even nunchuks. This place had just about everything a trucker could need.

A knife would probably come in handy, he thought; unfortunately, there was no one readily available at the locked display, and he didn't really feel like tracking someone down. Then he saw some knives hanging from their packaging on the wall. They were probably harder to steal being in the packaging so they didn't need to be locked up. He took a closer look at them. They were made by Kershaw; he seemed to recall that they were decent knives, so he grabbed one.

In the center of the store was a hot food section with hot dogs accompanied by some sort of taco things spinning around on hot rollers. The case next to it had burritos, lousy-looking chicken nugget things, and equally terrible-looking pizza slices. Another smaller case displayed hamburgers and cheeseburgers wrapped in golden tinfoil.

Cheeseburgers…If I never see another cheeseburger in my life, that'll be just fine with me.

He decided to pass on the hot food section, headed toward the front of the store, and grabbed a bag of chips, a couple of ready-made sandwiches that didn't look too bad, and a gallon of drinking water.

He brought it all up to the cashier lady, a plump, kind-looking older woman with her hair in a bun who was standing behind the counter. "Is that it, sweetie?" the cashier lady asked.

He found a bag of beef jerky conveniently displayed by the register and added it to the mix. "Yep, now it is… Thanks."

"The damage is thirty-five, forty-three," she said, as she started bagging up his stuff. "Credit or debit?"

"It's debit."

"There ya go. Have a nice day," she said, handing back his card and the receipt.

As he was putting his card and receipt in his wallet, the receipt caught his eye…another lightning bolt. *Am I really that stupid?* On the receipt was his name, the last numbers of his credit card, the time, and then the kicker, his location. *I most certainly am!* He was worried about his phone being on, and here he was, running his debit card in a store, not to mention at the gas pump!

He turned back around to the cashier lady. "Is there a bank or an ATM around here somewhere?"

"There's an ATM right at the back of the store, hon." She pointed in that direction.

"Great, thanks," he said, as he headed back. *Gotta hurry. They could be dispatching a cop to this place right now!*

He wanted pull out as much cash as he could but honestly didn't know how much that would be. He felt stupid for not being better prepared. He had seen on the internet some people who had whole bags packed full of stuff, food rations, cash, medicine, clothes, knives, guns, ammo, you name it, just in case they ever had to bail out quickly. They called it a BOB, or bug-out bag. It seemed a bit extreme and even sort of silly when he was reading about it then, but at the moment, it made a hell of a lot of sense. *Maybe I should have paid more attention to it all. Maybe I should have paid more attention to a lot of things.*

He slipped in his card and was able to withdraw five-hundred dollars from his checking account on the first shot. *Not bad.* He tried it again. *C'mon, hurry up, you stupid machine. Yes! Another five-hundred dollars!*

How about one more time? Nope. It wouldn't work a third time. He quickly tried from his savings account. *No? Why not? It's my money! How will I get my money out now?*

Oh well, I've got a thousand dollars. It'll have to do. Then, while passing the front of the store again, he saw prepaid Visa cards for sale. That would work. He looked at one and saw it could be good for anywhere from fifty to five hundred dollars. He grabbed two of them and hurried back to the cashier lady for one last swipe of his stupid and traceable debit card.

"How much you need on these, hon?" she asked.

He felt a little strange, like she might know he was up to something. "Five hundred each please," he said, trying to sound nonchalant.

"Okeydoke, dear," she said.

Didn't think a thing of it. Good!

She rang him up and out the door he went, carrying a plastic bag full of junk in his left hand and the gallon water jug in his right. He felt a little better getting that done.

As he stepped outside, he did a quick survey of the area around the gas pumps. *No cops.* He realized he had better go the other direction on the freeway now, because if he was being tracked either by phone or credit card, it would be pretty obvious which way he was going.

As he walked past the transient on the sidewalk, the man slowly stood up. "Hey!" he said. "You wanna sell that car?"

Dave quickly said, "Sorry, it's not for sale," and kept walking. *Like that guy's gonna have twenty grand in his pocket anyway.*

The man said loudly, "Hey, how abouts I just take it for a little test drive, ya know…Ya know what I'm sayin', brother?" and started following Dave.

Yeah, right. Dave now ignored the idiot completely. He didn't like the way this was shaping up in the slightest.

Maybe I should've bought a cheeseburger after all.

He thought about the thousand dollars cash he had in his pocket plus another thousand in the prepaid Visa cards. He had his hands full of groceries and was feeling pretty vulnerable at the moment. He felt a big lump in his throat. *This can't be happening.*

At another pump, a man about Dave's age was with his young son. They were filling up a minivan. The man gave Dave a look that Dave knew all too well. He knew it because he had used it himself; it was a look that meant, "This could be trouble for you, but I'm not getting involved, buddy. Sorry."

Those were the only other people out there at the time being. Dave kept walking toward his car. He just wanted to get in and drive away.

However, now the guy was getting even closer. "Just let me take it for a drive. I'll bring it right back, man. I promise, brother, c'mon."

Dave turned to look at him this time. The man was maybe thirty years old, skinny, with sores on his face. His cheekbones were practically popping through his skin. He looked like a crackhead to Dave. With his hat pulled low, Dave couldn't see his eyes too well, but he imagined they matched the few teeth he had—*yellow*.

One thing Dave learned from working the hotel desk is that druggies of the meth variety didn't like to make eye contact or small talk. They usually wanted to get away from people as soon as possible. Drunks, on the other hand, liked to hang around talking and carrying on all night, like lost puppies looking for their mother. Agitated, however, either could become unpredictably violent without much warning.

Dave tried to do his best to make this end well by using a term of endearment. "Sorry, buddy, maybe next time. I really gotta run, sorry." Dave turned back around and continued walking toward the car.

With a drastically different tone, the man said, "You ain't goin' nowhere, bro," and put his hand on Dave's shoulder from behind. That was a threat. No doubt about it. *Do unto others before they do unto you.*

Dave's right hand clenched hard on the water jug handle. He locked his wrist up tight and turned his head to measure the man up. Then, with all his might, swung around and—WHAP!—clobbered the freak right upside the head. It was a direct hit, rock solid and completely effective.

The sound was incredible, like a fat kid belly flopping off a high dive. The force was incredible too. It nearly knocked Dave off his feet as the jolt went down his arm and into his torso. When the momentum of his arm stopped suddenly, he nearly fell over but was able to maintain his balance.

Crackhead didn't fare so well. His hat went flying, his head followed, and his skinny body struggled to keep up. He fell against a gas pump, and desperately trying to keep his balance, he fell ass-backward over a trashcan and down onto the pavement. He was completely disoriented and hardly a threat at that moment. Dave wasn't about to stay for another round. It was time to get out of there while he had the chance.

The kid with his dad at the other pump yelled in amazement at what he has just seen, "Holy moley! Did you see that, Dad? That guy just clobbered that weirdo guy! Oh man, that was totally awesome! Did you see that, Dad?"

Amazingly, the water jug survived the impact. Dave fished out his keys and threw everything on the passenger seat as he got in his car. He was shaking and had a hard time getting the key into the ignition. *Just like at the airport.* He lined up the key with the slot slowly and jammed it in fully; turning it, the 340-cubic-inch V8 engine fired right up with a roar.

He threw it in gear and as he pulled out, glanced over at the little kid and his dad at the other pump. The kid had a huge smile on his face and was giving him a thumbs-up. The father's face combined a look of shock and satisfaction. Dave just looked at them blankly as he rolled by.

He took a last look in his rearview mirror. The dirtbag was still struggling to get to his feet. He looked similar to a man down on his hands and knees looking for a contact lens. Then he tried to get up and fell down again, like a drunk trying to find his feet. To say he'd had his bell rung was probably an understatement.

Don't meth up your life.

Dave drove out of there with his heart pounding. The adrenaline got the best of him, and he stepped too hard on the throttle, causing the rear tires to spin and squeal. He let off, took a deep breath, and did his best to drive out of there like a normal person. For all he knew, with the way he had haphazardly used his debit card, the cops were on their way right now.

Soon he was back on the freeway, heading west this time, back toward Mountain Home, Idaho, where he would have to stop and gas up again, this time paying in cash. He never saw one cop. The car seemed to be running well. He was doing seventy, and cars were passing him doing eighty.

Fine by me. No need to be the fastest car on the freeway.

He really didn't know where he was going to go exactly. *What's my final destination?* He did have an old friend out in Portland, Oregon, that nobody really knew or thought about, so at least that gave him a direction to go for now. What exactly would he say when he got there though? He couldn't just move in with an old friend that he hadn't seen, much less talked to in over two years.

What was he going to do? He wasn't really sure. He had no plan at all. *I'd better figure out something.* At this point, he would be considered an outlaw, right? Yet he had not been contacted by anyone from law enforcement. *I could just be out fishing or something. I could be on vacation as far as they know, right?*

He thought that maybe he should call the hotel and tell everyone he is taking vacation, just in case the cops started poking around there. *No, they've probably already been to the hotel looking for me.*

What a mess this was. He felt sick to his stomach again. His head ached with thoughts, none of which seemed clear. *Am I going to run into some weirdo at every gas stop?* This was two confrontations in two days. It was insanity.

He wondered how many outlaws were guys like him, where something stupid and out of character happened, and it all went terribly downhill from there. Someone accidentally hurt or killed somebody, and the fear of prison sent them running. *They couldn't all be terrible people, could they?*

Obviously, there were psychotics and crazy people, but he wasn't one of them. All he did was tackle a guy and, well, shove a cheeseburger down his throat. *But how did that kill him? He was alive when I left.*

That's right. He was alive when I left! Maybe someone else came along and killed him. The guy was alive when he left him there. Did that make a difference? He figured it didn't, as he couldn't exactly prove it anyway. *Hope the guy I just nailed with the water jug doesn't fall over dead.*

This was really getting out of hand. He felt as if he was living someone else's life. He had instantly become a different person entirely—a person he couldn't even relate to. *Was it murder? Am I a murderer?*

His dad's words from long ago swept across his mind. They had gotten into a small disagreement about Dave thinking about moving in with a girlfriend he had at the time. The girlfriend was a couple years older than him and had her own apartment. Seemed like a good idea to Dave at the time and a way to get out of his parents' house.

"You really think that's the right thing to do, Dave? You two planning on getting married?" his dad asked.

"No, we haven't talked about that. I mean, I haven't asked her or anything," Dave responded.

"Well, I am sure she will really appreciate that, son."

"It's not what you think, Dad. I just think it's better for us both financially. It's not about sleeping together. It's just kind of falling into place."

"Whatever you gotta tell yourself, I guess. I remember being your age. Good luck with the temptation, son. Just because something falls into place, doesn't mean it's the wise thing to do. I know everyone wants to learn the hard way, but believe me, some roads are easy to get on and difficult to exit."

"I know, but, it's just…you know, kind of a gray area and all."

"The gray areas are where you wipe your feet as you head toward the light. Look, Dave, it doesn't really matter if you flip burgers or own an NFL team. In this life, rich or poor, it all ends the same for everyone. What matters is your character, remember that."

Those were not his father's last words by any means, but they were the ones that stuck.

His dad saw things very black and white, and it was annoying at times, but you always knew where he stood. He made mistakes, but mistakes are different from deliberate actions.

The gray areas are where you wipe your feet and move on toward the light. His feet were definitely muddy now. He wasn't sure if it was even possible to wipe them off, or how to even go about it. *Forgiveness? Character? I wonder what Dad would think about my character now? Some roads are difficult to exit.*

As it turned out, the girl did not want him to move in with her anyway. Apparently, he wasn't her only boyfriend. That news was just plain humiliating.

He now realized that the incident at the airport, in fact, was not what caused all of this to happen to him. It was his secret relationship with Tina-Rae, the one he didn't tell his wife about. That was the root of all his problems.

He did like Tina-Rae; he really did. He would never cheat on Kat though, at least not in the way most people would describe cheating. He did cheat though, by dancing around in the gray area with Tina-Rae. The gray balls had caught up with him, rolling him over and exposing him. Then he boldly lied right through his teeth to Kathy. No wonder she could never look at him the same way again. He came clean, a day late and a dollar short, and only because he got exposed. That, then caused an intense anger in him that he could not control, and a man wound up dead.

It's not the obvious darkness that we know we should avoid. It's the gray areas that will kill you—white lies…excuses…rationalizations…character…gray areas.

He drove on, thinking about the man at the gas station and the man at the airport. *What is with these guys? Why were they both so bold? Why did neither of them fear him in the first place, or at least respect him?*

He must look like some sort of pushover or wimp. Maybe he should put on fifty pounds, shave his head, grow a beard, and dress like a biker. He could get him one of those goofy flat-billed ball caps the punks wore and some big hoops for his earlobes. Maybe if he looked more like a jerk, people would leave him alone. His mind raced on.

He wished he had never gone after that guy at the airport. He still couldn't explain how that happened—it just did. *The anger.* The gas station guy was different though and thankfully, was surely still alive.

He glanced over at the water jug on the passenger seat, grabbed the handle, and lifted it up; it was pretty heavy. *What does a gallon of water weigh, five pounds or so?* It felt heavier than that. He couldn't remember what a gallon of water weighed, but it sure packed a punch. *Eight pounds maybe?*

He thought about how the jug had impacted the side of that guy's scabby face. It seemed stupid, but he decided he didn't want to drink that water now. He didn't want that jug anywhere near his mouth. He figured he could pour it in his radiator if need be. At that thought, he checked his temperature gauge—all was well.

He set down the contaminated water jug and dug through the plastic bag of stuff he purchased from the truck stop store. He fished out the pocketknife. It would be good to have a knife handy at his next gas stop. It would be a bit more appropriate than packing around a water jug. He thought about the gun in the suitcase, then back to the knife.

It was encased in a clear plastic packaging that was not exactly easy to open. *I hate stuff that's packed like this.* Dave steered with his knee as he tried to open the package, first by bending it back and forth and then by trying to chew through it on one edge. He swerved slightly over the white line while being distracted by the stupid packaging. He soon figured out he'd have to open it later, and he set it down. *I need a knife to open my knife with. Ridiculous.*

28

Detective Carr answered his cell phone. It was the office. "Hello, Carr speaking."

"Hey, Matt, it's Ed. We got a coroner report back on Mr. Ronald Wells, your airport cheeseburger guy."

"Oh great, let's hear it."

"Um, let's see, blah, blah, blah…Oh, here we go… Time of death, approximately twelve thirty, June sixth… Cause of death is…Hold on, this is on a different form than they used before. Here it is…Myocardial infarction."

"A heart attack?"

"Yeah, Matt, that's what is says. Also, let's see, says small bump on head, not life threatening, and um…no air way issues. I guess despite the cheeseburger thing, it's just the heart failure."

"Heart attack. Twelve thirty. June sixth."

"Yep, that's it"

"All right, well that's interesting. Hey, I just thought of something."

"What's that?" asked Ed.

"Ronald."

Ed didn't understand. "Ronald? Ronald what?" he asked.

"Ronald McDonald." Matt laughed out.

Ed laughed also. "Nice, Matt, real funny stuff."

"I know it, what can I say? I'm hilarious."

"Sure."

"Well, thanks, Ed, I appreciate the call…pretty crazy news. I didn't suspect a heart attack, that's for sure. Oh hey, has anyone contacted his family?" Matt asked.

"Oh yeah, yeah, sorry. John tracked down an uncle. Said the uncle didn't seem too concerned about him being dead though. Get this, he just wanted to know how much shipping would be."

"Shipping?" Matt asked.

"The body…His uncle wanted to know what it would cost to ship the body."

"No way! Really? Shipping?"

"That's what John said. Funny, huh?"

"Yeah, that *is* funny. Sounds like this wasn't exactly his favorite nephew."

"Sounds that way all right. John didn't know what to say. He could call UPS, I guess, right? What…I dunno, five-foot-eight, two-hundred fifty pounds, how much?" He laughed.

"Yeah, no kidding, call UPS." Matt laughed himself. "Thanks again, Ed."

"Yep, you bet. Good luck, Matt."

"Thanks, Ed, have a good one."

"Oh wait!" Ed added. "I just thought of something else."

"What's that?"

"The Hamburgler!" Ed belted out.

Both men laughed aloud.

"This just keeps getting better. See ya, Ed."

"Yeah, later."

Matt hung up and shook his head in disbelief. *The Hamburgler, that's funny…and shipping. That is just strange.*

Wells died from a heart attack. That could actually be good news for Mr. David Preston, if he could find him. He obviously wasn't going to answer his phone. *Hope he's not on the run and about to do something stupid.*

Detective Carr was still angry about the story getting out.

29

Dave had to stop and fill up the tank again on the Plymouth. He had forgotten how terrible the gas mileage was on these old cars. Thankfully, this time his stop was uneventful.

He was on the west side of Boise, heading toward the Oregon border. Sagebrush behind him and in farmland now, he found himself speeding a bit and slowed down.

He also noticed a number of butterflies flying across the road, and he was getting quite a few of them with the windshield and of course, the grill. As he went farther, there were more and more of them; then there were literally thousands of them—small white butterflies all over the place, everywhere. There was literally a large cloud of them moving across the freeway. He was punching a hole right through this cloud and in his rearview mirror, saw the wound filling back in as more butterflies fluttered over the road. He had never seen anything like it. He was just plowing right through them.

It seemed strange; he was sure no one cared that he was running down butterflies, but he had accidentally killed one man and his life was forever changed to outlaw status, or it soon would be. How many butterflies equaled one man? You could kill a lot of butterflies and no one would think anything of it. *If you killed every butterfly on the planet, that would probably get some attention. What about mosquitoes…or cockroaches…or rats?*

The butterflies are innocent though. He started to feel bad about how many were skipping off his windshield as the powerful V8 pushed him through them. He saw a few of them actually go right into the hood scoop on the car—straight into the furnace, which was the engine itself. *Must be like hell in there to them. I wonder if they even feel pain at all?*

He knew he couldn't stop now. It was part of the deal. You don't stop for butterflies. Little things get run over by big things. That's just the way it goes. Big, uncaring, organized forces always run over anything in their path. That's what they're designed to do. That's the purpose—to get somewhere, no matter what's in the way. *Except I really don't know where I'm trying to get to.*

He was sure big things were going to be running him down soon. Large forces, government forces, the disappointment of his loved ones, the universal laws of God himself, he felt them all looming over him. What was it that they called it? *Impending doom.* Impending doom, it was inescapable and a certain eventuality. It was closing in on him. Just like the butterflies that survived, the next time they might not be so lucky, and the cycle would continue forever.

Such was his dream as a child; in his head, the little balls got run over by the big ones. The innocent being run over by the uncaring and unstoppable. *I'm not exactly innocent, am I?* He felt quite small and vulnerable. The thought of big forces coming after him was unnerving. How could he escape it?

Dave's mind wandered. He felt like he was trying to maintain his sanity as the Plymouth's engine buzzed in his head. The butterflies had trailed off, and now there were only a few stragglers flapping across the freeway. *Survivors.*

Where am I going? I'm going nowhere. What am I doing? I'm not really sure. It seemed everything was corrupt—every institution, every government, everything. All was all polluted, save for Jesus and perhaps puppies and butterflies. *Jesus. Can He help me now? Will He?*

He unzipped his suitcase and pulled out the handgun. Looking down at it, he remembered how it worked. It was simple really. He pulled back the slide and let it fly. It closed with a loud clack. It was so solid. He marveled at it a bit. Then it occurred to him that the magazine was in it. He had just loaded it, and there was the hammer, cocked, waiting, ready to fall!

What was I thinking? He panicked a little, not being as familiar with the weapon as he thought he was. His face became hot. He knew enough to know this could be a bad situation if he screwed it up. *What was I thinking!*

Okay, unload it. Just keep it pointed away and unload it. He pointed it toward the passenger floor and calmly pushed the magazine release. The magazine dropped out of the grip and fell in his lap. The hammer was there locked back and ready to drop. If that happened, there would be a loud explosion and an unwanted hole in his car. He could imagine how loud that could possibly be. *Loud, really loud.*

He looked up to make sure he was still straight on the road. He was steering with his knee and considered pulling over to deal with the gun. However, being parked on the side of the freeway would draw attention to him. He kept driving on with his knee and manipulating the Colt.

He knew there was a way to decock the hammer, but he wasn't so sure how to do it. Suddenly, this was starting to seem like rocket science after all. All he could do was pull the slide back again, which he did. The cartridge flew out of the gun and landed on the floorboard of the car. Again, the gun closed with a solid clacking sound. He would have to worry about that bullet later. He looked at the gun and pulled back the slide again, and again, making sure it was unloaded. *Empty?...*

Good. Then, pointing the gun away from him, he pulled the trigger and the hammer fell with an innocent click. He took a deep breath and slid the magazine, now with one less round in it, back into the grip of the gun. He put it back into the suitcase, and zipped it up. *Need to think things through next time!* Once again, he found himself amazed at his own stupidity. The last thing he needed was a self-inflicted gunshot wound.

The butterflies were far behind him, and the sun sank behind the horizon. Dave looked out his window, toward the mountains beyond the farmlands. Could he survive in the woods? At least it might delay the fate of getting run over by bigger things. He knew he couldn't be a mountain man. He was much too soft for that. He didn't even know how to hunt.

His dad could have survived in the woods, easily. He missed his dad; he was one tough old man. He wished he had learned more from his dad about hunting, fishing, and the outdoors, but he just was never much interested in it all. Truth was, Dave was just not of the same bore and stroke of his father and felt as though he was, perhaps, some sort of watered-down version of him.

What am I going to do? What about my job? How will this all work out? He needed a miracle it seemed, a way to start all over again. What he needed was to pull some billionaires' daughter out of a burning vehicle, saving the day. *They couldn't send a guy like that to prison.*

A 747 could go down, just out in front of him, crashing through a cornfield, plane parts and fire everywhere. There would be people screaming and flailing around. He would pull over and run straight at the disaster without hesitation. Jumping through flames and plane parts, he would single-handedly pull people out of the wreckage and chaos. Then he would run out of the smoke with a baby under each arm, taking them to safety. Bravely returning again to the wreckage, saving women and children, all while news crews filmed it all live. In an instant, he would become the bravest man on earth, a national hero.

Not likely. The fact was, he was part of the American system. The system of social security numbers, every law imaginable, and ultimately, total financial control over all its citizens. He figured you couldn't get out of the system even if you tried. If you did try, they would label you a pedophile or a dangerous cultist and literally burn you to the ground. You could ask the Branch Davidians about that, if there were any left alive, that is. It was completely hopeless, and Dave felt all of it creeping up on him.

30

"You got a girlfriend?" Trip asked Kyle

"Yeah, of course, she has no idea where I am now though. You?"

"Nah, well I did but nah, not no more."

The two were trying to calm their nerves before they carried out their plan.

"What kind of name is Trip anyway?" Kyle asked.

"It's not my real name. My real name is Tripoli."

"Tripoli? Like the city?"

"Yeah, I guess my mom thought it was cool or something. She thought it was in Italy."

"What?"

"My mom, she thought Tripoli was a city in Italy," Trip said.

"Where is it?" asked Kyle.

"It's in Libya, not Italy, but I guess the Italians ruled it at one time or something. I looked it up, so she was sort of right, I guess."

"Well, I agree, it's a pretty cool name."

They paused. Then Trip said, "I'd really like to see her though."

"Who?"

"My old girlfriend, I mean. Hey, man, I don't wanna die here. I really would like to see her or anyone."

"We're not dying here, dude, no way," Kyle said. "You wanna hear something messed up?" Trip just looked at him.

"Before all this, I was at home visiting my mom and my brother, ya know, and well, I got in a huge fight with my brother. What happened was, when I went to leave, I grabbed my wallet out of my bedroom and looked in it and I was missing a hundred-dollar bill. So I basically freaked out and went after my little brother, blaming him for stealing it, ya know, and um…he swore he didn't take it, but I knew he did.

"He wouldn't admit it, and he was crying. I was yelling at him. He's twelve, ya know? So my mom gets on him too, telling him to give it back. He keeps swearing he didn't take it. So I was really pissed now and just said to forget it and I took off with my car. You know, he is just crying and swearing he didn't take it. I just left. You know, after calling him a liar and a punk and everything."

Kyle's eyes had welled up as he continued. "So anyway, I get to a gas station and pull out my wallet, and the hundred dollar bill is in the pocket behind my debit card. I mean, I remembered putting it there, but I didn't remember that earlier when I thought my little brother took it for some reason. I just didn't remember, so of course I owed him a huge apology and everything. I mean, he thinks I hate him, and you know, he thinks I'm so cool and everything.

"Well I never apologized to him. I mean, I was going to, but I just didn't yet. I should have called him right then. I should have drove back home. I was only a few blocks away at the gas station. I mean, I'd give that kid everything I own if I could see him again, ya know? So yeah, I ain't dying in here, no way, man."

There was another pause, then Trip said, "When my mom got sick and died, I was just a kid. I don't remember her ever being really sick. I just remember her being in the hospital, but she was always smiling at me. I didn't really think anything was really wrong.

"When she died, we had a big funeral and all. I don't really remember it that well, parts of it, I guess. There was bunch of people I didn't know there and everything. But I remember driving back home with my dad. I remember it was strange, because now that my mom was gone, I was sitting in the front seat with my dad. I felt bad about it and told my dad that should probably sit in the back. He looked at me and then back at the road, and told me there are different kinds of people in this world. There are those that go through life, and there are those that live it. 'There are a few rare people,' he said, 'that don't just go through or live life, but that can actually feel it. Your mom was one of those special people that could feel life. You enjoy that seat, Trip.' So I stayed up front, feeling proud to be where my mom once was.

"I never really understood what he meant about feeling life, really. I pretended like I did. I really wanted to be like that. I just figured I wasn't like my mom. I couldn't do it like she could, but you know what, man? Right now, I feel you. I really do, man. I feel life. When we get out of here, let's go see your little bro."

"I'm determined," Kyle said.

"Me too, man, let's do it."

"Sorry about your mom too."

"Hey, Kyle," Trip said, "maybe we should pray."

"Um, yeah, right…maybe we should. Okay, you go ahead."

The two young men bowed their heads and Trip prayed. He hadn't prayed in a long time, but he was familiar with how his mother used to pray and the words that she used.

"Dear Lord, we come before you humbly and ask for your help. Please forgive us our trespasses. We ask that You might…"

Trip paused, realizing he couldn't pray like his mother, and went on using his own words.

"God, me and Kyle just ask that you help us get out of here somehow. In Jesus's name, amen.

"Amen," Kyle echoed.

Just then, they heard the barn door creak.

"He's coming, you ready?" Trip whispered

"Yeah," Kyle said, "I'm ready."

They got into position. The barn door opened fully, and Kyle listened closely as the man on the outside walked in. He thought he heard a light switch go on, but he didn't notice any change in the atmosphere. Then footsteps approached to the container door where he lied still just inside. The latch of the door was being opened! Kyle's heart jumped in his chest. He tried to find Trip's eyes with his, but it was still too dark in their prison. *Would Trip still go ahead with the plan? Would he? He had to. They both had to.*

Maybe it was a good guy out there, maybe they were being saved! The lever of the box was lifted, and the doors started to open, letting in a little light. Kyle looked at Trip, who was obviously as fearful as he was. Kyle nodded at him. Trip nodded back. It was now or never. They began to stand up. The door opened, and there he was, a giant redneck farmer, with shotgun in hand.

Kyle and Trip charged the door and surprised the man. He lifted his shotgun just as Kyle threw his handful of lime powder in the man's face, aiming for his eyes. Then Kyle grabbed the shotgun and tried to wrestle it from the hands of the giant. A familiar smell ravaged his nostrils—*alcohol.* Trip attacked the man and tried to knock him over, but he may as well been trying to move a mountain. Trip put everything he had into trying to tackle the farmer, but he didn't move him at all, not one inch.

The man lifted his arms straight up, violently and easily ripping the shotgun from Kyle's hands. Then he brought the butt of the gun down on top of Trips head. Trip fell to the dusty barn floor with a thud. Trip was out cold, just like that.

Kyle scrambled toward the open barn door. He could see outside. Grass, trees, freedom! *What about Trip?* He'd have to come back for him with the cops later. That was the agreement: if one of them got free, just go. Run and keep on running. He was going to make it! *Faster, faster, faster!* He was nearly out the barn door! He could see a hill in the distance and trees. There was an old rusty Ford pickup out there. His legs were firmly under him, and he was on his way, nearly home free!

A sonic boom erupted in the barn behind him, and suddenly he saw his own foot in front of his face. He was looking right at his own shoelaces. *Strange,* he thought. His body lifted off the ground, and he fell violently onto his back. Did a bomb go off? Frantic, he tried to get up but his leg wouldn't work after one step, and he fell down on one knee. *What had happened?* He looked at his leg, as he tried dragging himself out the door. His pants were shredded. He was starting to bleed from his left calf. That big psycho had shot him! He tried to stand up, but fell again. He tried dragging himself the last few feet out the barn door. He just had to make it out there and into the sunlight, if it was the last thing he did.

Then the man was over him with the shotgun barrel pushing his face into the dirt.

Kyle couldn't breathe or speak. *Please don't kill me*, he thought. *Please don't kill me.* He lay lifeless and powerless. His life flashing before his eyes, he thought of his mom, his dad, his little brother. He hoped they were all okay. His old girlfriend, he even thought of his dog. He closed his eyes and tried to accept the fact that he was going to die here in this terrible farm-prison. So much for praying, they were never going to get out of this place. It was over.

The man took the gun off the back of his head and then grabbed him by his shirt, lifting him easily off the ground, pulling him across the barn floor. His leg suddenly hurt like nothing he had ever felt before. Throbbing in pain, soaked in blood, his calf was full of shotgun pellets. He felt dizzy. *Am I dying?*

The kidnapper was spitting lime powder out of his mouth. It was bitter and clumpy. He grunted and cussed. He pulled Kyle over to a workbench where he grabbed a roll of duct tape. He dropped Kyle face down into the dirt and taped his arms behind his back. Then Kyle screamed in pain, as he started taping up his wounded leg.

"Shut up, dummy!" yelled the man. "You ain't dead yet, but you will be!" The big psycho then took the tape and wrapped it hard around Kyle's mouth and head. Kyle gasped for breath. He breathed in hard through his nose, trying to stay alive.

The man left him lying there in the dirt and walked over and picked Trip up off the floor. Trip quietly moaned, blood and dirt covered his face.

"And you is next, dummy!" the man yelled, as he effort-lessly tossed Trip back into the iron box with one arm. Then he closed the door.

31

Dave kept driving west with the same thoughts going through his head, over and over again, as they had done all throughout the day. Mostly he thought about how he hated everything about, well, everything. He had known of people in terrible circumstances who could still somehow find hope; as for him, he just couldn't drum any up.

It was pitch black and beginning to rain. His headlights were practically useless. The constant droning of the car motor began to take its toll as well; he was beginning to feel weary behind the wheel. Worse yet, he was starting to see things that weren't there. People on the side of the road, cars in his blind spot, things on the road in front of him that he knew didn't exist. He was seeing ghosts of both human and animal form. He rolled down his window to try and get some fresh air. The rain was entering the car too easily though, so he rolled the window back up.

What is that!? He swerved to miss a shadow image of what he thought was a dog running out in front of him across the road. *I'm gonna have to pull over. I can't drive much further like this.* He drove on at a slower pace looking for an exit; anywhere he could hide off the road for a while would do. He just needed to rest for a little while.

32

Genius Gary was in his dirty kitchen, which smelled like stale beer and mold. He was so angry. That dum-dum Kyle kid had tried to poison him by throwing that crap powder in his mouth. He filled his mouth with beer and spit it out in the filthy sink. He wiped his face off with a dirty dishrag and threw it across the room. He was done with this place! The time had come. He taped up the kid's leg pretty good to keep his blood from falling out. He wanted the blood to fall out, but not here. When people saw blood, they took you seriously. He needed to let the blood spill somewhere else.

He grabbed his note and his trusty shotgun and went back out to grab Kyle from the barn. He still tasted the powder in his mouth, even after chugging the rest of his beer. *That kid was gonna pay dearly for this—with his life.*

He opened the barn door, and Kyle was right where he left him. He grabbed him by his arms, dragged him out to the truck, and threw him in the back.

He closed the barn door, jumped in the truck, leaned over, and made sure his big knife was in the glove box— it was. He started up the truck and headed out toward Interstate 84.

He would just find a spot on the side of the freeway and do what he had to do. Someone would find the kid soon enough. As he got closer to the freeway, he noticed it was starting to rain. For some reason, he thought that the rain was bad. Why was it bad?

The note! If it got wet, it would get ruined! The side of the road wouldn't do. He had to find somewhere dry. He knew just the right place. It was perfect, actually. It was a little farther down the highway then he had planned, but it was perfect. He started humming a song to himself. "And bingo was his name-o!" That was a good song.

He reached over and pulled open his glove box, where a bottle of Vodka also resided. He grabbed it. "Time to celebrate, Gary. You have done well," he told himself. He unscrewed the top and chugged on the bottle until his throat burned, and the clear liquid ran down his chin. He stomach warmed up. His time had finally come. It was all going his way. Nothing could stop him now, nothing in the world.

33

Dave finally pulled off the freeway to a rest area. He drove around to the back end of the parking lot where he would be away from the lights and the restroom building. It wouldn't be easy catching much sleep in the car, but he was definitely tired and needed to rest as best he could.

He grabbed his phone off the passenger seat and found himself tempted to turn it on. Instead, he leaned his seat back as far as it could go, and sooner than expected, he dozed off in a light sleep.

He found himself outside by a lake, with a gun in his hand—the Colt 45. A large bird was at his feet. It looked like a bald eagle, and it's lying dead in the dirt. *Did I shoot an eagle? Why would I shoot an eagle? Maybe it's a duck. No, it's obviously an eagle. Damn!*

Sure enough, as should be expected, up drove an Idaho Fish and Game officer on a four-wheeled ATV. He looked down at the eagle and then directly at Dave, and said, "This means trouble, you know?"

"I thought it was a mallard," Dave responded, trying to sound as innocent as possible.

"A thirty-pound, white-headed mallard, huh? Interesting," the officer retorted.

Dave had to admit. It did seem ridiculous. *I'm going to be in big trouble over this.* He stood speechless while the officer just glared at him.

Then, remarkably and unbelievably, the officer suddenly sped away on his ATV without saying another word. *Wonder what that was about. Where is he going?*

Then he saw the answer. An American Indian was riding toward him on a large brown horse. He looked like a Comanche or maybe a Navajo. *No, it's Comanche. I'm sure of it.* It's an incredible sight. He's one lean, mean, fighting machine, that's for sure. He had a war-torn, sunburned face, with a large scar starting at his forehead and running all the way across his left eye and into his cheek. His eyes were dusty brown, like his horse. He had long dark braids of hair hanging all the way down to his chiseled, bare chest. There were beads tied into the braids and a bird feather tied at the end of each braid. *They look like eagle feathers. Great!* How he wished he'd killed a duck instead. He tried to will the dead eagle into a dead duck, but it didn't work.

The Comanche's face and body are painted with what Dave can only assume were berries and perhaps blood. His legs were bare; he had black and red stripes painted down the most impressive thigh muscles Dave had ever seen. Not the kind of bulky muscle a bodybuilder had, but lean, usable muscle. The kind of muscles that served a purpose far beyond entertainment or simple vanity. In one hand, he held the reins of the horse, and in the other, he gripped a long spear.

Dave looked at him with astonishment. This was one impressive human being, a warrior in every sense of the word. *What's he doing here? Is he going to kill me? He looks like he wouldn't think twice about doing it.*

He jumped off the horse with ease, right in front of Dave, his bare feet hitting the dry ground solidly. He looked Dave in the eye and then down at the dead eagle on the ground.

Dave was speechless. *He's going to put his spear right through me!*

To his relief, the warrior stuck his spear in the ground and knelt down next to the bird. The bird then simply got up and walked. Then it jumped up and grasped the Indian's forearm with its huge, sharp talons. The claws dug into the man's skin, but it didn't seem to bother him at all. As the Indian stood up, the bird let go and flew off. Dave watched it effortlessly lift off and fly away, looking completely healed; for that, he was thankful.

When he turned back, the Indian was on his horse, riding away. Dave ran after him. "Wait, wait!"

The Comanche stopped, looking at him calmly.

"How did you do that to the eagle?" Dave asked.

"Fate," was the response.

He had to mean faith, not fate. He healed the bird with faith somehow.

"You mean faith?"

"Fate," was again the response.

Fate? What does that mean? Maybe he's confused between fate and faith. The Indian then turned his horse and kept riding on. More warriors like him appeared, seemingly from nowhere, and followed him. There must have been twenty of them. *A war party?* They were equally as impressive as their leader. They were similarly decorated and apparently returning from battle. Not one of them looked down at Dave. They just followed their leader. *Is he some sort of spirit guide...a war chief...or maybe both?* They sped up and rode away out of sight, their horses kicking up a large cloud of dust.

"Wait!" Dave called out as he ran after them

They were moving along good now, and he couldn't catch up. *My bike! Of course!*

He ran over to get his Kawasaki Ninja; it was right there in the back of the garage. It's a bit dusty from sitting so long, and Dave prayed the battery isn't dead. He pulled in the clutch and pushed it between the garage wall and his roommate's 5.0 Mustang, trying not to hit either one, and on out to the driveway. He jumped on, pressed the switch, and it fired right up!

Awesome. I'm so glad I still have this thing after all these years! I thought I sold it. I must've just forgotten about it. He took off after the dust cloud the horses were kicking up. He caught up easily, passing the ones at the rear of the group and moving quickly toward the leader. *I've got to talk to him!* He looked over at their horses. Impressive as they were, they can't match the speed of the ZX-7, not even close. *I bet they've never seen anything as fast as this! These guys probably don't even know the Japanese exist, much less make machines like this, yet they don't seem all that interested. That's strange.*

He saw the leader up ahead, the miracle worker. He's getting close, then the bike sputtered and died. *No! What's going on? Out of gas? You have got to be kidding!* He twisted the throttle all the way, but nothing happened. He pushed the starter button, again and again, but the pistons never fired back to life. It's dead. The bike slowly coasted to a stop as the Indians pass him again.

Dave continued to yell toward the leader, "Wait! Wait!"

The last one in the group, knowing Dave's desperation, stopped and looked down at him. Dave looked up and saw the Indian had bright blue eyes, very familiar. He felt he was experiencing a déjà vu. *Have I seen this man before?*

The black-and-white-spotted horse he's mounted on stood silent with its head down. The Indian was younger than his leader. He looked to be maybe only eighteen years old but just as dangerous as his elder. He had long black hair, and half his body was painted black from his head to his feet. Dave noticed a deep cut across the man's chest, and his torso was caked in dried blood. Some of the black paint, or whatever it was, had rubbed off in places, showing the skin underneath. Like the others, it seemed as though the young Comanche had been to hell and back again, numerous times, and came out victorious.

Though it appeared he'd just killed one hundred men, his face was strangely calm, even friendly. "The fate is yours, Dave, not the eagles," he said.

Dave was completely confused. "What do you mean?"

"Freedom, that is your fate," he replied.

Freedom from what? Death? Dave looked at the warrior blankly, still not understanding.

The Indian sensed it and spoke again, "Freedom from fear. No man in fear is free."

Dave looked again at the gash in the native's chest; it's starting to bleed. He wondered if the young brave was going to die. He didn't want him to die.

Then Dave noticed his father standing there, right in front of him.

"Dad, what are you doing here?" he asked

"It's good to see you, son," his dad said. Then he reached out his right hand which was clasped around something. He opened his hand, with his palm facing up. In his hand were three white butterflies. They were just standing there on his palm wings slowly fluttering. Dave didn't understand and looked into his father's eyes looking for an explanation. *Were they angels?*

His father said to him, "Don't forget, Dave, never forget." Then the three butterflies flew off of his dad's hand and hovered in front of Dave.

"Father," his dad said, and as if commanded, one of the butterflies flew toward Dave's head. It then somehow entered his forehead and went right into his mind.

The next butterfly flew right at Dave's chest and like the first, somehow disappeared into his chest and into his heart. He felt his heart jump.

"Son," his father said.

The last one flew toward his right hand. Dave reached out and like his father, opened his hand palm up. The butterfly landed softly on his hand. It sat there with its wings slowly flapping.

Dave looked at his dad again.

"Holy Spirit," his dad said with calm and confidence.

Dave closed his hand around the butterfly. He looked up and his dad was gone. He opened up his hand, and the butterfly was gone too. It had entered his body, just as the others had done.

The young Indian was still there, looking curiously down at Dave. Dave's attention turned toward the wound on the warrior's chest. The wound was bad and bleeding even more now. It would likely kill him. It would surely kill him.

The warrior looked at his wound also. Even though it was severe, it seemed to cause him no pain whatsoever. However, it seemed the Indian knew the injury would be his ending. He put his hand on it, and in checking it, accepts that it's fatal.

With a steel gaze from intense blue eyes, he looked directly at Dave, making sure of eye contact.

"We know what we are." Then he asked, "What are you?"

34

What are you? Dave jolted awake with a rushed intake of breath. It took a few seconds to get his wits about him.

Father, Son, Holy Spirit? Mind, heart, hand? Thoughts, intentions, actions? Never forget.

He sold that Kawasaki motorcycle over fifteen years ago. Where was he? Slowly it came to him. He was in his Plymouth, at a rest stop in Oregon. He couldn't have been sleeping for more than ten minutes.

Freedom from fear? I'm definitely living in fear. How could he be free, with all that had happened and all that was coming his way? It was coming. He felt it more than ever now. He reflected on everything that had just happened, or *seemed* to have just happened.

What am I? It was a good question actually. Being from a dream, he knew it was he himself who was asking it.

Had he acted too hastily? *What am I he going to do, really? Be a convict on the run...the next face on America's Most Wanted?* The more he thought about it, the more foolish he felt. *I can't live like this. I can't leave Jessica this way. How will I ever see her again. What would Kathy think of me now? How can I ever do anything, ever again? I need to tell her I love her.*

It was an accident that the man at the airport had died. Truly, it was just a terrible accident. He'd probably made the biggest mistake of all by running; it made him look guilty. Well, he was guilty, sort of, but now he wasn't even free; he was fearful. Fear was shaking him to the core of his being. It had become him. *Freedom from fear…that's what I need. How?*

He sat up and turned on the phone. His heart was beating hard in his chest as it booted up. He prayed silently for God's help, although he had no idea how God could help him now.

When the display came up, he saw missed calls from Jessica and some number he didn't recognize. *And what's this one? A missed call from Kathy?*

He also had text messages. At the top of the list was a message from Kathy. With a lump in his throat, he opened it.

> Dave, please call me as soon as you can. We need to talk. Love, Kat.

Love? Kat? That was his name for her and his alone. In back and forth texts while they were separating, she signed "Kathy" or left no signature at all. He read it again, "Love, Kat," and had a hard time keeping it all together. He felt as if he might cry.

He looked at his phone for reception bars. *Not very good. Being tracked. Could care less…doesn't matter. It's over.* He stepped out of the car, trying and get better reception. The raindrops were small and cold. He pulled his hood up over his head and walked up a sagebrush hill at the end of the parking lot, behind his car. A single bar appeared on his phone.

He took a long deep breath. His hand was shaking as he dialed to call Kat.

She answered instantly, "David! Oh my gosh! Where are you? Are you okay?"

He didn't know what to say; he could hardly breathe. "I'm okay."

"Where are you, Dave? There's been a policeman looking for you, and you're all over the news..."

All over the news...Where is she...in Boise? "What do you mean 'all over the news'?"

"It's everywhere, Dave! Cheeseburger killer!" Her voice was shaking. "Dave, is that you?"

"Kat, I didn't kill anyone. I mean, I didn't mean to. It just was..."

She was crying. "Oh, David, they're looking for you! It's all over the news, the internet, everywhere! It was you at the airport, wasn't it! Oh my God, David! This cop from Boise is trying to find you! He called Jessica. He called—"

"Kat, I didn't mean for the man to die. I just tackled him and left him there. I promise."

"Where...are you... now?" she asked, sobbing more than speaking.

"Kathy," he said steadily. "Listen please..."

"Okay."

"I found out he'd died, and I got scared and left town. I didn't know what to do. I know what to do now, okay? I'm fine; everything will be just fine. You call that cop and tell him I'll be back in town soon. He can find me at my apartment tomorrow morning. I'll be there, I promise. He can even call me tonight if he wants. You tell him that, okay? Will you do that for me?"

"Okay, Dave, I will. I'm just so glad you're okay. I love you, Dave. I am so sorry."

"I love you too. It's going to be okay."

He saw lights flash and noticed a truck pulling into the rest area, an old pickup. It stopped right in front of the bathroom. *Just a guy needing to use the bathroom.* Dave continued reassuring Kat, while casually watching the pickup truck.

A big man got out of the truck, carrying something. *What is that in his hand? A knife…I don't know.* The man went to the back of the truck and pulled open the tailgate.

"Oh no! God!" Dave gasped

"Dave, what is it? Dave?"

Dave crouched down, watching the man at the truck.

"Shhh…hold on…"

"Dave, what is it?"

He ignored her.

"Dave?"

"Wait, Kathy, please…"

The man pulled a body out of the back of the truck and began dragging it toward the bathroom.

Dave couldn't believe what he was seeing!

The legs of the body kicked and twisted in unison; they were tied together.

Whoever it is…is still alive. Probably not for long. "Kathy, I gotta go." He hung up and shoved the phone into his pocket.

The man was almost to the door of the bathroom building. Dave could think of nothing to do but yell as loud as he could.

"HEY!"

The man startled and turned toward him looking for where the sound came from. He left the body in front of the door, then went back toward his truck, and opened the door. He threw in whatever he was carrying before and then reached further into the cab of the truck and emerged with a rifle in his hands.

Oh no, he's got a gun!

He didn't see Dave up on the hill. Dave was now lying on his belly next to some sagebrush, watching the man. The ground was wet but firm.

The man was just twenty yards away at the car, looking into it. It was dark, but Dave could see he was a large man, very large. The man looked up and stared into the darkness, trying to locate the person behind the shout.

Dave felt the vibration, like an electric shock, before the sound rang out. *The phone!* The man turned toward the sound and started toward it, gun raised to his shoulder.

Dave crawled toward the other side of the hill as fast as he could, phone still ringing in his pocket. He fished it out and threw it as he rose to his feet in a frantic run.

The shotgun went off.

BOOM!

The sound ripped through the cool night air.

Dave twisted, lost his balance, and fell on his back in the wet dirt. *I've been shot!* He scrambled to his feet again, left arm dangling, running down the other side of the hill away from the man.

The shotgun sounded again, this time from farther away. Dave heard the pellets cutting through the air. He tensed up his body for the impact. The pellets hit the bushes five feet to his right.

Thank God! Can he still see me?

Dave tried to stay low as he scampered to the left, through the taller sagebrush at the base of the hill. *God, save me!* He moved more slowly now. It was pitch-black down in the low place, but he could see the man at the top of the hill looking around, mostly in the wrong direction.

He doesn't see me. Thank you, Lord.

The phone rang again where it lay in the dirt. The big man walked over to it and stomped on it. It stopped ringing for good. The man continued to look around.

Dave stopped, waited, watching the man, trying not to breathe heavily, his heart thumping in his chest, *Quiet!* he told himself as he peered through the branches of a large sage.

Dear God, help me. Please help me. He kept the man in sight, while creeping slowly away. His left arm was numb and useless, blood dripping off his fingers. The left side of his back penetrated by twelve-gauge pellets stung badly, a throbbing sharp pain.

The man walked a loop around the top of the hill, paused, and then started back toward the parking lot.

Dave circled along the base of the hill, staying low behind the brush, trying to keep his eyes on the big man with the gun.

The man paused again and looked into Dave's car, then continued toward the body squirming under the lights of the restroom building.

Dave knew what he had to do, and he didn't hesitate. He ran as low and as fast as he could toward his car. His left arm dangled loosely as he ran.

Please, God, help me.

The man approached the body, gun raised.

Dave reached the car and opened the passenger door of the Plymouth. The door latch clicked when it opened, and the interior light came on.

The big man noticed and immediately turned around.

Dave reached inside, pulled the suitcase off the seat, and scooted behind the car for protection. Unzipping the case was no small task, with only one working arm, but he managed to get it open far enough to slip his hand in. Instantly he felt the cold steel of his father's Colt 45. He pulled the gun out and sat with it on the side of his car. The ground was wet and cold.

The man with the shotgun approached.

His father's words pierced through his mind. *An unloaded gun is nothing but a fancy paperweight.*

It wasn't unloaded entirely, but there was nothing in the chamber ready to go. Dave was sure of that. He thought about his incident in the car when he struggled to make the gun safe once again and wondered how many rounds the magazine actually had in it now.

No idea…no cartridge in the chamber…a paperweight.

He had to get it loaded and quickly. His left hand useless, Dave tried to rack the slide by pressing it against his leg and pushing forward on the grip; it didn't work.

The man was getting closer.

Dave slid back the other way as a shotgun blast pocked the Plymouth's bright-orange paint.

Dear God, help me! It's do or die!

Lying almost completely on his back, scooting around the car with his legs pushing him, Dave put the slide of the gun between his teeth and clenched down as he pushed the grip forward. The metal slipped between his teeth and he felt them chipping. He bit down as hard as he could and pushed forward harder, finally overcoming the strength of the recoil spring. The slide snapped forward. He tasted the saltiness of blood in his mouth.

Ready to go. Dave lifted the gun.

The man appeared at Dave's feet, shotgun shouldered.

Dave pulled the trigger.

CRACK! A giant light flashed before Dave's eyes, the man's body spun.

BOOM! A shotgun blasted toward the stars.

Dave's own weapon nearly flew out of his hand. He was able to hang on and control it, as his life depended on it. His ears rang as he tried to stay focused on what was going on before him.

The big man jerked around again. He pumped the shotgun and brought it down pointing at Dave.

Dave pointed back and quickly pulled the trigger again.

CRACK! Another beautiful ball of blue fire left the end of the handgun.

Dave saw the man's giant body against the night sky, standing perfectly still.

Besides the high-pitched ringing in Dave's ears, all was silent.

The shotgun slowly slipped from the big man's grip and clattered onto the pavement. His head tilted over to one side. Then his body fell in what seemed in slow motion, yet in full force, against Dave's car, and into a giant lump on the pavement at Dave's feet.

Dave pointed his gun at the large mass, waiting for movement, but the giant lump never moved again.

He took a deep breath and silently thanked God it was over. He then felt something warm and wet moving under his leg. *Blood…lots of blood.* He strained to get on his feet and started making his way toward the restroom building. His left arm now throbbed with pain, and his right arm sagged from the weight of a handgun that seemed to get heavier with each step. It felt as if he was carrying a bowling ball. He was breathing heavy, and the cool air burned his lungs. His mind was still racing, but his body was sluggish. He approached the figure on the ground. Ears still ringing, he looked into the eyes of a teenage boy who lay there under the lights. *Those eyes... They were just like the Comanche's eyes in the dream, but they weren't blue. They were brown, yet still bright.* Dave tried to put it all together. *What exactly is going on here. Am I dying?*

His mouth taped shut, the boy couldn't speak, but gazed up at Dave. His eyes spoke volumes to him.

This kid has been through a lot. Now it's over. It's going to be okay. It's over.

Dave was dizzy, ready to fall over. His head felt like a balloon about to pop. The ringing in his ears seemed to be getting louder. He slowly lowered himself down next to the boy, let go of the gun, and went to work, as best he could, tearing the tape off the boy's wrists.

Once his hands were free, the boy quickly tore the tape off of his own mouth and took in a large breath of air and spoke, "Did you get him? Is he dead?"

Who is talking?

Dave's world was becoming increasingly dark; he lowered himself on down to the concrete.

"Is he dead?" the boy asked again louder.

Dave heard him this time.

"Yeah, I think so," he answered in whispered voice.

"Who are you?" asked the boy

Me?

"I'm no one. Who are..." His voice trailed off.

"Kyle."

Kyle. Dave repeated the name to himself, as he lost consciousness. The boy spoke some more, but Dave didn't hear him.

Kyle looked the man over and found his left arm side and back had multiple wounds. The arm especially was bleeding pretty badly. Quickly, but carefully, he unwrapped the tape from his ankles and wrapped it around the man's arm, up as high as he could. He tried to pull the tape as tight as he could. He needed to stop that arm from bleeding.

It wasn't working. He needed to make it tighter. He picked up the gun and looked at it. The slide was locked back; it was empty. He pushed the magazine release and the spent magazine fell out. He took the magazine, put it under the tape on the man's arm, and used it to twist the tape tight. It was all he could do to turn it one full revolution, but it was tight enough now.

He looked at the man who had just saved his life and wondered if he was going to make it. He hoped he would. He had so much to tell him and to thank him for. Trip was still over there in that box. He couldn't wait to tell Trip what had happened, but he would have to.

Kyle sat holding the makeshift tourniquet so it wouldn't untwist, and there he sat, and there he waited.

35

For I know the plans I have for you, declares the
Lord, plans to prosper you and not to harm you,
plans to give you hope and a future.

—Jeremiah 29:11

Monday, June 8

———————————————————

A game show host was talking. "Looks like you figured it
out, Dave!"

Dave looked up at him. He's sitting atop another man's
shoulders. He's a shorter man sitting on the shoulders of a
taller man.

The taller man didn't speak at all. In fact, the shorter
man on top put his hands over the taller bottom man's
mouth, then moved them up to his eyes, then to his ears.
He repeated this; put his hands over mouth, then eyes,
then ears. He kept doing this over and over, like some sort
of ritual.

It reminded Dave of a little plastic figurine he had as
a child. The figurine had three monkeys that were stacked
up on each other's shoulders, just like the game show host
guys. The monkey on top had his eyes covered; the middle
one, his mouth; and the one holding up the other two, his

ears. At the bottom were the words "See No Evil, Speak No Evil, Hear No Evil." Each monkey had his own pose.

In this case, the man on the bottom has to do all three it seems...or the guy on top is doing it for him.

Does the man on the bottom have arms?

Yes.

Why doesn't he just cover his own eyes, ears, and mouth?

Oh, he's using his arms to hold on to the smaller man so he won't fall off. That makes sense then.

Apparently, Dave had figured out the riddle of the man riding on the other man's shoulders and now was part of the game show. The host was the shorter man. He and the taller man led Dave through a door and into the game area. Dave looked around.

This place looks like the YMCA near my home. I've been here before.

There were two large swimming pools. People were going about their business swimming, and kids were jumping off diving boards. Some old people were doing some sort of exercise class at one end of the pool.

The short man, atop the taller man's shoulders, spoke again. His voice was very excited and loud. *He plays the part of game show host well. Can any of this actually be real? It seems pretty out of place! I don't remember anything on my schedule about being on a game show. That seems like something I would remember. Where is my phone anyway? Oh yeah, it got stomped on. I need a new one.*

"Prizes, prizes, prizes!" the man exclaimed, and the crowd roared with cheers. Dave couldn't see where the crowd was, but apparently there's quite an audience.

A girl appeared and started showing Dave the prizes he could win. She showed him a card with a picture of some waterfront resort hotel.

"A grand vacation to Cuba!" the man proclaimed. The crowd roared again.

Cuba? Dave tried to act excited and smiled at the girl. She motioned to a poster on the wall. Dave saw a picture of some rock band with long hair, guitars, and snarls on their faces. *Who is that?*

The man exclaimed loudly, "Second prize! A weekend concert for all your friends with"—he took a deep breath—"Megadeth!"

The crowd went nuts. This time, Dave noticed some of them looking through the windows from the outside.

Megadeth…Are they still around? He looked at the poster again, and sure enough, it said "Megadeth" on it. The faces on the poster were actually moving. *Strange…must be some new technology.* He went up and looked at it. *It's paper-thin. It even has a tear in it, but it's electronic?*

He touched it, and his finger went right through it. It's like a thin sheet of liquid. He pulled his finger out and it's dry, but the hole remained. *Oops! Maybe you're not supposed to touch these things? This isn't like anything I've ever seen before. How was I supposed to know?*

He wondered what would happen if he poked a hole through one of their faces. *Better not.*

A light shone down from the ceiling, circled around the floor, and then stopped on Dave and the game show host. The girl walked away to a wall with three doors in it and stood by the wall in the pose of a mannequin. *Maybe she really is a mannequin. It's hard to tell.*

A hush fell over the building. The shorter man stopped moving his hands over the mouth and ears of the taller man, put them over just his eyes, and held them there. Dave sensed that the taller man was excited to see what will be next but had to have his eyes covered for now. *It's all for building drama, I guess.*

"And now for the grand prize!" the shorter man shouted. "Are you ready?"

The crowd roared, "Yeaaah!"

He repeated, "Are you ready!"

"Yeaaahh!" they roared even louder.

The shorter man lifted his hands off the taller man's eyes and shouted, "A new car!"

The crowd went nuts, lights flashed, spotlights circled, and then shone down on the new car. The taller man motioned for Dave to have a look. Dave turned his head and saw a Volkswagen bug at the bottom of the swimming pool. *That seems like a weird place to put a new car.* Actually, it looked like a bug from the '70s, hardly new. *What kind of game show is this?*

As the crowd roared, Dave spotted the mannequin lady, leading Jessica and Kathy into one of the doors in the wall. *I guess she isn't a mannequin after all. She wouldn't be able to walk…more like a robot lady of some sort.*

There were three doors where the robot took Kathy and Jessica. *It makes sense now. All of this is to distract me from seeing where they're hiding Kathy and Jessica. I can't believe my luck. I've spotted them. I know what door to choose!*

I know this game too! All I have to do is pick the right door. I don't even care about those other prizes. I'm going to get my family back. Right here, right now! He walked toward the three doors and looked back at the game show hosts.

"Pick a door, any door!" the shorter man said. "Pick the door containing the item worth the most, and you not only get the prize behind the door but the new car as well!"

The item worth the most…worth the most to who? Doesn't matter, I don't care about the stupid car anyway. It's not new anyway. He looked at the doors again. *Where did it go?* He wasn't sure why, but one of the doors had disappeared. The one his family went behind was still there and looked just like it did before, but the only other remaining door was now outlined by flashing lights. It also had an armed guard posted by it. The guard was just standing there like a statue, AK47 slung over his shoulder, guarding the door. The rifle had a red tip at the end of the barrel.

I'm pretty sure that's an airsoft gun. That's weird.

Dave looked at the windows. The crowd was yelling and screaming for him to choose. He saw the fat slob from the airport, looking in the window, mustard on his beard. *He isn't dead after all. Is this all some elaborate scheme to separate me from my family? Of course! That's it! They want me to pick the fancy door that would separate me from Kat and Jessica forever! The game show host guys are evil. This whole place is evil. It's so obvious now. The only people who need to say they aren't evil are the evil people themselves!*

Since one door had already disappeared, Dave's afraid his door was going to disappear too. He wasted no time and started toward the door that he saw Kat and Jessica enter. The mannequin-robot lady was standing between him and the door. He took a closer look at her. *It's Tina-Rae. Is Tina-Rae a robot?*

She smiled at him and said, "Open the door, Dave," and stepped aside. Her eyes were reassuring. *Maybe she isn't evil, and she doesn't look like a robot. She seems to want the best for me.*

He suddenly felt very happy and confident. He nodded at her, smiled back, and reached for the door handle, but there wasn't one! *What? It was just there!* He fumbled around trying to find a way into the door. He tried to get his fingers into the edge of the door, but he couldn't do it. He began to get frantic.

There's no way in! He looked to the game show hosts for help. *I know they're evil, but they seem to be in charge. Maybe they can help.* They're gone. *Everyone's gone!*

He's completely alone now, still trying to open the door. *What the hell is going on here? Is this some sort of sick joke? A dream? A dream…It's a dream! It has to be. I want out now. Right now. I can wake myself!* He struggled to wake up. *Besides, I'd better get going to school. Oh man, no time to shower. I have to get going!*

Wait! What classes do I have today. Where are they? What time? Oh man, I'm going to be late anyway. I'm going to fail science.

No! Wait! Wait! I'm old enough to drive now. I can drive to school. Good! He ran to the garage and tried to get all the junk off his car. *Why's all this crap on top of the car anyway?*

High school. Why am I going to high school? I graduated last year. Am I some sort of loser still hanging around? I don't really have to go. I've already done this. I've got my diploma. I've already graduated. I've done this already. Why do it again? It makes no sense at all.

Wait! Is Kathy here? Maybe I'll see Kathy in the halls. How is Jessica born already if Kathy is still in high school? I don't even go to the same school as Kathy. Why are there no parking spaces at this stupid school? I'm going to have to park over by the football field.

"Mr. Preston?"

This isn't high school…

"Mr. Preston?"

Where am I?

"Mr. Preston?"

This is my hospital room. He tried to put the dream out of his mind and directed his attention to the person speaking to him.

"There's someone here to see you, Mr. Preston," the nurse said with a smile and motioned toward the door. A man wearing a cheap suit walked in. Dave didn't recognize him. The nurse left the room and then shut the door behind her.

"Well, well, well, if it isn't the world-famous cheese-burger killer," the man said jokingly.

Dave didn't really think it was all that funny.

"Wow, look at this place," the man said.

Dave looked around the room himself—everywhere, there were flowers, cards, balloons, and even stuffed animals. *Where did all this stuff come from? I don't even know this many people.*

The man stepped forward and stood just a couple feet from Dave's bed.

"I've been wanting to talk to you for some time now, Mr. Preston."

Dave just looked at him, not knowing how to respond. He was still dazed from his dream and now, his present reality. *Who is this guy?*

"I'm detective Matt Carr, with the Boise Police Department. I talked to your wife last night. She said you would be home today. Looks like you didn't quite make it though.

"I, uh, I meant to, I really—"

"I'm joking. It's okay. You had one hell of a night last night, huh?" He said as he pulled out a piece of gum, unwrapped it, and put it in his mouth. He looked around and not seeing a trash can, put the empty wrapper back into his pocket.

Last night? Dave was still trying to separate dreamland from reality. *Gunfight at a rest stop. That kid…all taped up… bloody…Kyle…His name was Kyle.*

"Oh, yeah, I guess I did. That kid, is he okay? Is he—"

Carr interrupted, "Probably best if you don't talk right now. Okay?

Dave nodded. *This guy is going to arrest me now.*

"But yeah, the kid's okay. Shotgun wound to his leg, pretty bad, but he'll be all right. You might not be here yourself if wasn't for him. An Oregon State trooper stopped by for a bathroom break and found him sitting there, hanging on to a duct tape tourniquet he'd put on your arm.

"He's okay, along with six other kids the Oregon troopers found at that guy's farm. FBI and everyone are out there now, I guess. You know the guy you had the Wild West shoot-out with? He kidnapped a bunch of kids, I mean, a bunch of 'em. That kid with you was just one of seven. You're really lucky he didn't kill you. The guy was not messing around."

Dave looked him in the eye, as if to ask a question.

"Yeah, he's dead. One of those shots went right through his neck and severed his spine, killing him instantly, no doubt."

Dave just stared at him, through him. He felt like the room was tilting somehow.

"He was a real bad guy. Had those kids all locked up in shipping containers, you know, those big steel ones. A couple of kids he apparently forgot to feed were barely alive. There were a couple girls from our neck of the woods too. Two teens we thought drowned in the river last week. They are all safe and sound, thanks to you."

I remember those girls being on the news. They got lost on the Snake River. Seems that 727 crashed after all…and there I was.

"Oh, and there was that guy at the airport."

Dave felt himself turning white with guilt. He looked the detective in the eye again.

"He'd robbed a little old lady and left her for dead, but we found her in time, also thanks to you. In some sort of crazy roundabout way, I'd say.

"Oh, and by the way, nice touch with the cheeseburger thing, but it didn't work. The guy died of a heart attack."

Heart attack?

Dave couldn't believe his ears. He stirred in his bed a little and found himself speaking out. "A heart attack?"

"Yeah, a heart attack. Unfortunately, your incredible timing, or dumb luck, whatever it is, doesn't get you off the hook. I wish it did, believe me, I do, but there are some things we need to talk to you about. I suspect you might want to be getting a lawyer. I think that should be no problem. It seems they're clamoring all over each other to represent you. Like vultures, I tell ya."

The detective pulled another piece of gum out of his pocket and threw it in his mouth. He went on.

"We'll be talking later about what happened. Let's just say I'm not here on police business at the moment, but I'll be back. You aren't going anywhere."

Dave looked at him. "I guess not."

He's going to arrest me later.

"Anyway, Mr. Preston, I wanted to slide in and thank you for what you did last night. Kid said he heard you yell out to draw attention to yourself at the rest stop. A pretty brave thing to do. You seem to have a knack for being in the wrong place at the right time.

"Oh, and by the way, it's illegal to have a gun in the passenger compartment of a vehicle in Oregon, and Idaho too, for that matter. Thank God you did, though. Otherwise, Oregon was about to have a real bloody mess on their hands, a real mess."

The detective paused and looked around the room, trying to take it all in. The room was literally stuffed to the ceiling with gifts. "Well, looks like you'll have public support, that's for sure. I'll be on my way now. Let's keep this conversation between us, okay?"

Dave nodded in agreement.

"Take care, we'll be talking later. You've got much more important visitors out there wanting to see you. Nice family by the way, take good care of them." With that, he smiled and slipped out the door.

Nice family? Jessica and Kat walked in; Dave couldn't believe what he was seeing.

"Dad!" Jessica screamed as she ran to the bed to give him a hug. He leaned into her as best he could, putting his chin on top of her head.

Kathy approached the bed with tears in her eyes, which brought tears to his. "Oh, Dave, did you hear about all those kids? You saved them all, Dave."

Dave just looked her in the eyes and squeezed her hand. Her eyes were clear and bright.

Jessica popped up abruptly. "Oh, Dad, you wouldn't believe how many people are outside the hospital wanting to see you! Oh my gosh, it's crazy. We almost couldn't get in! There are cops and everything. You just wouldn't believe it! There are news people out there and everything. The cops won't let them in, or they can't come in or I don't know. How is your arm?"

"They say it is going to be okay, honey."

"Oh good, I can't believe you got shot! I mean, really, can you believe it?" Jessica was obviously excited. Dave and Kathy looked at each other and smiled.

"Did they tell you will need a surgery on your arm?" Kathy asked.

"Yes, later today, I think," Dave responded. It felt so good to be talking to his wife again.

"They told me it would be later today, yes," she said.

The nurse knocked on the door and poked her head in. "Excuse me, Mr. Preston. There's someone else who would like to see you, if that's okay?"

"Of course."

She held open the door and nodded. A lady pushing a kid in a wheelchair came in, followed another younger boy. Kathy and Jessica backed away from the bed as they came forward.

He was all clean-shaven and cleaned up, but Dave recognized him instantly. *Those intense brown eyes.* It was Kyle.

"Hello, Kyle."

"Hi, Mr. Preston, this is my mom and my little brother Max."

Kathy, Dave, and Jessica all introduced themselves.

Kyle's mother walked up to Dave's bed, put her hand on his shoulder, looked him in the eye, and said quietly "Thank you, Mr. Preston. I can't thank you enough. I really don't know what to say, but God bless you." She had tears welling up in her eyes.

Dave smiled at her and nodded.

She wiped her eyes and then turned toward her younger son Max. "Max would like to say something to you as well, I believe. Max?"

All eyes were on twelve-year-old Max. He looked nervous but was determined. "Um, Mr. Preston, I just wanted to say thank you."

Dave smiled at him.

Tears suddenly ran down the boy's face. "Thank you so much for saving my brother's life!"

Max ran up to the bed, threw his arm across Dave's neck, and hugged him as best he could.

Dave put his good arm around the boy, hugging him back. "He saved my life too, Max. You take good care of him and your mom, okay?"

"Yes, okay, I will." He got up, wiped his face up as best he could, and went back by his brother and mom. Their mom put her hands on the little boy's shoulders and squeezed them gently. She then shifted them over to Kyle's wheelchair handles. "Well, we better go, boys, and let Mr. Preston be with his family."

"Okay," Kyle said, "we'll see you later, Mr. Preston. Take care."

"You too, Kyle, thanks. Come back and see me later if you want," Dave said.

"I will. I'm just right down the hallway. I think I get to go home tonight though."

"That's good. Take care…and thanks, Kyle," Dave said.

"Thank you too, Mr. Preston," Kyle said.

"It was nice to meet you all," Kyle and Max's mother said, and she spun Kyle around and pushed him back out the door.

"Bye, Mr. Preston, you're the coolest person ever!" Max said, and he followed his mom and brother out.

The nurse smiled at them with tears in her eyes also and then went out as well. She closed the door gently behind her.

Dave and Kathy were silent, enjoying being reunited. Jessica was silent also, at least for a second or two.

"Oh my gosh! Was that Max kid too cute or what?"

Dave and Kathy laughed.

"Oh, I almost forgot," she said, reaching into her jacket pocket. "Your neighbor Amy, remember her? Her and her mom, I mean, her aunt, are out there, and, um, she saw me and gave me this card to give you. Cool, huh? Open it!"

"Could you open it for me, sweetheart?" Dave asked.

"Yeah, of course!" Jessica sat on the bed with him and tore open the envelope. "Oh, I guess it's not a card," she said.

Inside the envelope was a little folded piece of paper. Jessica pulled it out.

On the front of the paper, it said "START HERE" and had an arrow pointing to the flap to start unfolding the paper.

"Okay," Jessica said, and unfolded the first flap. Written next, with an arrow pointing to another flap, was "KEEP GOING." She did.

"ALMOST THERE" and another arrow. Jessica smiled and unfolded it.

"ONE MORE" was written on the last flap. She unfolded it and flipped it over to reveal the full size paper. It read,

MY HERO!

Jessica grinned. "That is so cool!"

Dave looked at his family, his wife and daughter; they were both so happy. It felt so good to be back. He was no hero, but he knew what he was.

END

The word of God is living and active. Sharper than any double-edged sword, it penetrates even to dividing soul and spirit, joints and marrow; it judges the thoughts and attitudes of the heart.

—Hebrews 4:12